Other books by
JEAN FERRIS

Amen, Moses Gardenia

The Stainless Steel Rule

Invincible Summer

Looking for Home

Across the Grain

RELATIVE STRANGERS

JEAN FERRIS

FARRAR   STRAUS   GIROUX

NEW YORK

RELATIVE
Strangers

AUTHOR'S NOTE

I've taken considerable liberties with airline schedules for the convenience of this story. Anyone hoping to duplicate the flights taken in Relative Strangers *should consult with a travel agent, not a writer of fiction.*

To all those I love—
with hope that I'm doing it well

RELATIVE STRANGERS

1

*T*here were two letters in the mailbox when I got home from school, one for me and one for Lily. My friends think it's odd that I call my mother by her first name, but for my whole life it has been just the two of us doing things the way we wanted, and most of the time, I liked calling her Lily. It was okay with her.

Both letters were in the same handwriting—strong and distinctive, black ink, real fountain pen. Los Angeles postmark. Letters from my father. I stood, weighing my letter in my hand. It was heavy enough —good vellum has heft, you know—but not as heavy as I imagined it should be, weighted as all his communications were with things unsaid. Such as why he didn't call or write more often, why he didn't want to see me regularly when he was only a hundred miles away—in car-crazy Southern California, this is considered just up the road from San Diego, where I live— why my birthday cards were signed in handwriting other than his own (Lily guessed his secretaries did it and that's why the handwriting changed from time to time), why the expensive Christmas gifts were sometimes for a child younger than me and sometimes for one who lived a life that wasn't mine. The purple satin gloves and evening bag, for example. They weren't quite the thing for dishing up yogurt at Yogurt City, or wearing to school or on my occasional—very occasional—dates to the movies.

I put Lily's letter on the hall table and took mine into the kitchen. The cats, Madge and Wuffums, came to twine around my ankles while I looked into the refrigerator. I had a fantasy that someday I would find it furnished like a major appliance ad—a whole turkey, a ham decorated with pineapple slices, parfaits in fancy glasses, aspic salads—beautiful and orderly, although these were things Lily and I probably wouldn't want to actually eat. The surprise of it, the escape from everydayness, that's what I was interested in finding. Instead, I saw the same old stuff through that open door: milk, apples, furry leftovers, peanut butter, a bottle of chutney that was probably ten years old, and rolls of film. Yet every day I opened the

4

refrigerator with the same sense of anticipation. Maybe today the miracle would happen.

I hoped I had learned not to do that with my father. There wasn't going to be any miracle where he was concerned. Seventeen years of infrequent visits, usually involving a lunch of stiff conversation and long silences, had taught me that. But even though I might be seventeen on the outside, inside there was still a treacherous little kid of four, or seven, or ten who kept hoping her daddy would show up and love her so much that he wouldn't want to go away, regardless of the fact that the last time he'd seen me had been three years ago.

I took peanut butter, crackers, a knife, and the letter to the kitchen table and constructed my snack, with the help of the cats, before I read the letter. I liked to give myself time to prepare for a confrontation with my father, even a written one, so I didn't feel blind-sided, the way I usually did when I saw him in person or when I talked to him on the phone, which wasn't quite as rare, but was always unexpected. A continual frustration, that's what dealing with my father was, and I couldn't for the life of me figure out why I kept wishing for more from him.

I ate my crackers, lightly garnished with cat hair, then opened the letter.

April 25
Dear Berkeley,
I have a proposition for you. It seems to me you're   5

getting ready to graduate from high school, isn't that
right? I find myself having to make a business trip to
London and Paris in mid-June and am hoping that
you'll come with me. Let it be my graduation present
to you. I've come to think it's time we spent more time
with each other. I very much hope you can arrange
your schedule so that we can have nearly two weeks
together.

Oh, I have recently remarried and would like for
you to meet Paula, my wife.

I look forward to hearing from you.

Your father, Parker Stanton

Well. Blind-sided again. The offer of two weeks
traveling on insurance-company business with this father I hardly knew, who had signed this letter to me
with his full name, who had remarried and mentioned
it to me as an afterthought. It would be like taking a
trip with a total stranger.

I thought of calling Lily at the paper where she was
a photographer, but decided against it. She was often
out in the field, anyway, and if I had her paged, she'd
worry. She'd find out soon enough. This was Wednesday, the night we both stayed home for Shovel-Out-
the-House Night: household maintenance and catching up with each other. Besides, she had a letter of her
own from Mr. Parker Stanton, and I don't deny, I was
plenty curious about that. Especially because the
child-support checks and any communication my fa-

ther needed to have with Lily had always come from a lawyer's office. I have to say he's never been late with a support check, but that's probably because it's the lawyer who's paying attention to when it needs to be written.

I was at the kitchen table doing my homework with the cats tiptoeing over my papers, sparring with my book pages and chasing my pencils over the edge and onto the floor, when Lily came home. She staggered through the front door with two bags of groceries, reaching the kitchen counter just before she dropped them.

"Why do those baggers always put every single can in the same bag? And all the time they're doing it, they're chatting away with me, so I don't notice. God, I think I have a hernia. And there's another bag in the car, my little angel cookie."

"You only call me angel cookie when you want me to do something you don't want to do. Besides, look at Wuffums." As if on cue, Wuffums had curled herself cozily into my lap. "It would be a crime to disturb her."

"Well, you better get ready to call the cops. This is your mother speaking, the one who works hard all day to afford those diamond tiaras and polo ponies you have to have."

"Oh, okay," I said. I handed the cat to Lily, who sat down with her in the chair I vacated. Grumpily, Wuf-   7 fums rearranged herself in Lily's lap and sighed noisily. "See?" I said. "Poor Wuffums."

Lily stroked Wuffums. "Poor Wuffums," she agreed. "Such a tough life the old thing has." As I headed for the car and the last of the groceries, she called after me, "Any mail?"

"Yes," I yelled back. "Wait a minute."

I brought the grocery sack into the kitchen and began unpacking it. "We both got letters from my alleged father."

"Really?" she asked, her eyebrows lifting. "Not from the lawyer?"

I brought her her letter.

"Even in high school, he had the handwriting of an executive," she said, looking at the face of the envelope. "So strong and self-confident. That was one of the things I loved about him when I was seventeen and too impressionable to have been allowed out without a keeper." She snapped the rubber band around her wrist. She was trying to quit smoking and she was supposed to do this every time she wanted a cigarette.

Lily didn't seem in any hurry to open the letter. Finally she sighed and carefully slid her fingernail under the flap. She read, frowning, and then looked up at me. "He wants you to go on a trip with him?"

"Did he tell you where?"

"No. Just wants me to encourage you to do it. He must really want this if he's willing to write to me about it. Where?"

"London and Paris." I kept a straight face, not wanting to influence her reaction by my own. What did she really think about this offer? What did I?

"Wow," she said.

"It's a business trip. He wants me to go with him as a sort of graduation present. Almost two weeks."

"Two weeks," she said. "Double wow. Do you want to go?" She fingered the rubber band.

She wasn't giving me any help. I couldn't tell what she thought. "Why should I?"

"To get to know him in a broader sense?"

I could feel my four- and seven- and ten-year-old selves, with their daddy longings, stirring around inside me. I shook my seventeen-year-old self. "He got married again. Did he tell you that in his letter? Recently, he said."

Lily snapped the rubber band. "No, he didn't tell me. But it took him long enough. Maybe he'll be better at it now."

The kitchen was quiet. "This is the first time you've heard from him in years. How can you be so calm? Why don't you hate him?" I asked.

Lily stroked Wuffums. "Oh, I did hate him at first, when he took off and left me, eighteen years old, with no job, and a baby I didn't know how to take care of. But later I understood better how scared he was, and how overwhelmed. So was I. But having a baby means something different to a woman than it does to a man, I think. At least in the beginning. After all, Mother 9

Nature designed women to carry and bear and nurse babies. It makes sense there's something more between a mother and her child than there is with the father. That's how it was with me, anyway. Nothing could have made me leave you. And if something had, I certainly would have made more of an effort to see you than he has."

It pleased me to hear the breath of bitterness in what Lily said, to know that his conduct had marked her as well as me, no matter how fair she'd tried to be.

"So what do you think about the trip?" she asked again.

"I probably haven't spent the equivalent of two weeks' time in his company in my whole life."

"Probably true," she said.

"Not even Europe's enough to compensate for that." I crumpled my letter in my fist.

Lily opened my hand, took the letter, and smoothed it out on the table. "Do you want me to go?" I asked. She was being suspiciously noncommittal.

"I can't make this decision for you," she said, continuing to smooth the letter. "But think about something. He *is* your father. The only one you'll ever have—"

"Not if you and Grady get married," I interrupted.

Grady Bookwalter was a colleague of Lily's at the paper. Sometimes he took me with him and Lily when they went out, and he could ask the best questions. Maybe it was because he was a reporter, but no one else had ever asked me such interesting questions, like how would my life have been different if I'd been born blond instead of brunette. Or if I had a million dollars that I could spend only on charity, what would I do with it? Or what was the first thing I'd do if I became Queen? He liked my answers, too. And he was funny. He saved odd newspaper items for me, like the one about a bar losing its liquor license for waking up passed-out customers so they could order another drink. If he'd ever asked me what I thought the ideal father was like, I would have said him.

"Don't start that," Lily warned me. "Grady and I are just friends. But even if I should remarry, you'd have a stepfather, not a biological one—"

"Grady, even as a stepfather, would be a better father than Parker Stanton ever was," I said, interrupting her again.

"Berkeley," Lily said, giving me what she called her Eye of Doom, "forget St. Grady the Pure for a minute. Here's a chance to get to know your real father, the one you used to be so obsessed with."

I pushed my chair back and began to pace around the kitchen. "Would *you* want to take a trip with a total stranger?" She didn't answer. "I don't even know what a father's for, anyhow. You always told me the two of us made a whole family, and I believed you. I still do. Give me a good reason why I need him."

"There are different kinds of need," she said. "Sure, you can live without him. But you'll always   11 wonder about him. Won't you? Be honest. Some of your genes are his."

"Just one or two, I hope. The rest are yours and ones I've invented myself."

"All right, okay," Lily said, holding up one hand. "How about if we drop this discussion now and go on with Shovel-Out-the-House Night. Let's let our unconsciouses do some work. They know things we don't. We'll talk again at dinner tomorrow—and not before. Deal?"

"I don't know what else there is to talk about, but okay, if you want to." I wasn't at all sure I wanted to hear from my unconscious.

"All right." She stood up. "I'm cooking tonight."

"I saw the cartons from the deli," I said.

She shrugged. "Dinner is dinner."

I needn't have worried about hearing from my unconscious. My conscious was trouble enough. The more I tried not to think about my father, the more impossible that became. By the end of the evening, I had a tidy room and a pile of clean laundry, but a very messy mind.

I lay wide awake in bed, staring at the ceiling. I'd gotten along fine without him. Sure, Lily had loved him once, when she was seventeen and dumb enough to get pregnant and then marry somebody who didn't want to marry her. I wondered why she'd loved him in the first place. What would it take for me to fall in love now? Or could you even control who you fell in love with? I had the idea love was some sort of irresistible force, like a big wave at the beach, that just hit you and knocked you flat whether you were paying attention or not.

Was there a reason I loved Lily, or was it just habit? No, I loved her because she listened to me and laughed with me and did hard things to make life better for me, like going back to school while she worked two jobs so she could get a better-paying and more interesting job. She helped me solve problems and liked my friends and told me things I didn't want to hear when she thought I was doing something that wasn't good for me. I still think she's wrong about not letting me buy the motor scooter, though.

I got out of bed and went down the hall to Lily's room. She was sitting up in bed talking on the phone.

"Okay, but I'm having dinner with Berkeley first. How about if I call you when we're finished. Okay. Good night."

"Who was that?"

"Nell." Nell was the science writer on the newspaper, and Lily's best friend. "We're going out tomorrow after you and I have dinner."

"Is Grady going, too?"

"Yes, Grady, too. But we're not going to the Elvis Presley Wedding Chapel. Just the movies."

"Darn." I got into bed with Lily with my back turned to her. I don't know why, but it's easier for me to talk about hard things if I don't have to look at anybody. I squashed the pillow into the right shape under my head.

"Mom," I said. My voice came out in a whisper. "Were you ever sorry you had me?" I heard the snap of the rubber band.

"Only when you leave wet towels on the bathroom floor and don't clean out the cat box." Then she scooted down in bed, hugged me from behind, and said into my ear, "Never, never, never. Not for a single second. I didn't have to have you, you know. But you were mine from the minute I knew you were on the way. The timing was wrong, the situation was bad, nobody was happy about it, but you were mine."

"Were you really in love with my father?"

"Madly. As you only can be at seventeen. He was the handsomest thing I'd ever seen, and he said he loved me, too. And I really thought we were going to go to the same college and then get married and live happily ever after."

"Maybe you would have, except for me."

"Maybe. But you were the test of our characters and he flunked. Sooner or later he would have, anyway."

"You didn't get to go to college at Berkeley the way you wanted to."

"I still got my Berkeley." She squeezed me. "And I got to college eventually. So did he. It worked out."

"What did you love about him?"

"Oh, the wrong things. He was gorgeous and fun to

be with and smooth-talking. And he had lovely manners. All that's fine, but now I think the most important quality in a man is a willingness to negotiate with you, to work with you to improve things. Back then, I'd never even thought of that. Nothing seemed more important than having a good time with a great-looking guy."

"Why did you get married? It wasn't such a big deal then, was it, not to?" Sometimes I wondered if it would have been easier for me if my parents had never married. Then I wouldn't feel responsible for their splitting up, and maybe, too, I wouldn't have expected anything from my father. If he couldn't have made any sort of commitment to Lily, I might not have expected him to make one to me. But he did make one to her, at least for a little while, however insincere it might have been.

"Maybe not, but it was to me. And it wasn't just because I was pregnant. I was in love. I'd already thought about being married to him. He was reluctant, but I leaned on him and cried and made him feel guilty. I don't want him to seem like the villain here. I shouldn't have forced him. But I believed in happily ever after then."

"Don't you anymore?"

"Now I think of it in a different way. Then I thought of fireworks and walking on air and perfect understanding without having even to talk. Now I think it's muddling along together, sort of the way you   15 and I do, with love and loyalty and the desire to keep muddling."

"Doesn't sound very romantic."

"Not to you, maybe. It sounds terrific to me. And it's not so easy to find, either. Believe me. Well," she amended, "there'd still have to be a few fireworks. And a tiny bit of walking on air."

"Did you miss him when he left?"

"Well, sure. Plus I was hurt and mad as hell and feeling sorry for myself and so busy with you and finding a job that I was just one walking blob of misery. I called him and wrote him and cried and cried, but he just kept saying he couldn't do it. And he was telling the truth. He really couldn't. After a while I calmed down and realized what I actually missed was what I wished he was, not the real him. And I certainly didn't want to be with somebody who didn't want to be with me. Still, it was a long time before I wanted to even talk to a man again."

I don't know why I'd never thought to ask Lily these questions before. Because I tried not to think about my father, I suppose. One of the other things I loved about Lily was that she told me the truth. She wasn't above evading an issue, but if I asked the right questions, she'd always give me the truth as an answer.

"Do you think he's a bad person?"

"I don't know what he's like now, of course, but even then I didn't think he was bad. He was young and
selfish and probably weak. He felt cornered and

wanted out. So he didn't do it gracefully. He seems to be doing well now. He'd have to have been living in a cave not to have learned *something* in the last seventeen years. Could be that's why he wants to take you on this trip."

I snorted.

"Come on. People show different sides of themselves to different people. He might be different with you now that you're more grown up than he was with me." Lily's voice quavered.

I turned around and looked at her. Her eyes were wet. "What's wrong? You should have told me if you didn't want to talk about him."

"It's not that," she said, sniffing. "I guess I'm afraid."

"Afraid of what?" I handed her a Kleenex from the bedside table. Her fear frightened me.

"Afraid that if you go on this trip you'll fall in love with him, like I did, for the same reasons. After I've done all the grownup and responsible child-raising stuff, he'll get your love without having to do anything."

I hugged her. "Oh, Lily, that'll never happen. You and I have years of memories I'll never have with him."

Lily hugged me back. "I'm glad to hear you call me Lily again. You only call me Mom when you're feeling especially insecure and upset."

"Lily, Lily, Lily," I said, hugging her harder.

17

2

The next evening Lily put a platter of burritos on the table, sat down, and said, "Well? What did your unconscious come up with?"

"Nothing. I guess I'll have to take it in to the shop. Yours always works better than mine."

"That's because I'm not afraid of what's in mine."

Lily took a burrito and began piling it with lettuce, cheese, salsa, sour cream, guacamole, and black olives. "Wouldn't the American Heart Association have a fit if they could see this?" she asked.

"I could turn you in to them, you know."

"You little fink," she said, taking a big bite and rolling her eyes in ecstasy. "I dare you to eat one of these after saying that."

"No problem." I loaded sour cream on my own burrito. "Your secret's safe with me."

Lily patted her mouth with a napkin and said, "Okay. Here's the verdict of my unconscious. I have to say, my conscious doesn't like it so much, but the old unconscious thinks you should go." She put the napkin down. "Sorry. That's what it says."

"But why?" My voice rose in a perfect four-year-old whine. Some things you never forget. "I don't want to go."

"I know you don't. But, number one, the man *is* your father. You need to know him better or you'll always wonder what he's like, whether you'll admit that or not. You may make him into something he never was, the way people elevate their dead relatives to sainthood just because they're dead, no matter what they were like when they were alive."

She had something there. I'd fantasized all kinds of reasons for my father's neglect of me, from amnesia to a tender wish not to disrupt my life with Lily to a cruel streak a mile wide. "You said number one," I said, stone-faced. I wasn't liking this. "Is there a number two?"

"Number two is, you have the opportunity for a great trip. Even if you don't get along with him, you'll still have gotten to see Paris and London. Maybe it's   19 wish fulfillment, but I've never been there and I'd love for you to see those places for me. And the chances of me being able to afford to take us there the way he will are nonexistent."

"But I don't care about seeing Europe. And how do you know how he'd take me?"

"He always liked things classy—just look at his stationery and those expensive gifts he sends you, even if they are inappropriate. Part of what he didn't like about being married to me—not that he tried it for long—was that we were too poor and couldn't afford nice things. Our apartment was full of hand-me-down furniture and he said he'd rather have no furniture than what we had. But me, hey, I was just glad to have something to sit on and eat at and sleep in. I didn't much care what it looked like. That made him wild, too, that I didn't care more. If he's still the same, and I'm betting he is, at least about that sort of thing, then he'll take you traveling first class."

"That doesn't matter to me. I know people who've traveled with backpacks and slept sitting up on trains."

"So do I, but they didn't have a choice. You do. There's a number three, too. That is, I think it would be good for you and me to spend a little time away from each other. You'll be leaving in September and I know UCLA isn't that far away, but I also know you're not going to be coming home every weekend. I need some practice at being separated from you."

20   "I've gone to camp. I've stayed overnight with

friends. I went to Mexico for a week with my Spanish class. What's the big deal about a two-week trip?"

"You know what I mean. The two of us have been so close for so long. Now we need to get used to being apart."

Well, maybe she was right about that, but I didn't see why we couldn't do it when I left for college. Why now? I'd just come back and we'd get used to each other again and have to go through the same thing all over in September.

"I hate to even ask," I said. "Is there a number four?"

"There is, but you might not like it."

"I haven't exactly been crazy about the first three either, so what are you worried about?"

"I'm probably a lunatic for even thinking this way."

"What could it be?" I asked. "Now you have to tell me."

"A million parents would hate me if they could hear this," she said, sighing. "Well, you've always been such a sensible kid, with a minimum of experimenting and testing your limits—and mine. It might do you good to spend some time with somebody more flamboyant than me. Give you a little balance. Stretch you a bit."

Oh, she had me there. I knew I had the spirit of a lioness, I could feel it in me. But I seemed to have the heart of a rabbit. Nobody could talk me out of doing something risky faster than I could myself. And then

I would berate myself for not being more of a risk-taker. I always felt as if I were trying to break through a barrier and never quite making it.

"Couldn't I just start knocking over liquor stores or sky-diving instead of going to Europe?" I asked, my rabbit heart winning once again over my lioness spirit.

Lily laughed. "Sure. When do you want to start?"

I shook my head. "I'm almost afraid to ask. What's number five?"

Lily snapped her rubber band. "There isn't any number five. Or maybe that's the part of me that wishes he'd stayed as remote as he has been up to now." She rubbed her wrist. "Your turn."

I made designs in my sour cream with the point of my spoon. "I don't know if it's my unconscious or not, but this is what my head says. He's ignored and neglected me for my whole life—I've been nothing but an incidental afterthought to him—and that's made me sad and angry and confused. Just because he shows up now with what I see as a bribe is no reason for me to change my mind about him."

Lily leaned forward. "And your heart? Does it have anything to say?"

I had to look down at my plate to blink back the sudden mortifying tears. "My stupid heart says I've always wanted to have my daddy to myself for a while, even if it's only for two weeks."

Lily reached across the table and took my hand.

22   "Then maybe it's time your heart got its way."

3

May 1
Dear Dad,

Thank you for the invitation. Yes, I accept. I applied for a passport today. I graduate June 14 and I can have two weeks off from Yogurt City where I work, so let me know when you plan to leave.

Sincerely, Berkeley

P.S. Can you come to my graduation?

May 5
Dear Berkeley,

I was so pleased to get your nice letter, and more

pleased to know that you'll be able to come with me.
I've made our reservations for June 15. If this doesn't
give you time to get ready, please let me know. We'll
return June 27. I can teach you some tricks about jet
lag to lessen the pain when you have to go back to
work. I've done it plenty of times myself.

I'm sorry I won't be able to make it to your graduation, but I look forward to seeing you the day after.

With love, Dad

May 8
Dear Mr. Stanton,

I don't feel right calling you Dad anymore when
you can't even be bothered to come to your only
child's high school graduation. Just because you
signed your letter with Dad instead of Parker Stanton doesn't mean   And you might as
well forget about me going on that trip with you
because

May 8
Dear Mr. Stanton,

I don't feel right calling you Dad anymore when
you can't even be bothered to come to your only
child's high school graduation. I wanted to call off
the trip, but Lily won't let me. She says I made a
promise and I have to keep it. This just shows you the
difference between what a good parent acts like and
the way you

May 10
  June 15 is fine. Should I bring anything special?
                                              Berkeley

May 15
Dear Berkeley,
  The only special thing I can think of that you might want to bring is an umbrella, since, unlike Southern California, it does rain over there in the summer. Also, any cosmetics you especially like or medicines you take, since we might not be able to find them there. Comfortable walking shoes, of course. Other than that, we can buy you anything you may need along the way.
  I'm enclosing your ticket from San Diego to Los Angeles for the 15th. I'm sorry it's so early, but our flight to London leaves at 11:00 and we have to check in two hours in advance. I look forward to the 15th.
                                      With love, Dad
P.S. Could you send me one of your senior pictures? It's been longer than I thought since I last saw you and I know how fast girls your age can change.

May 19
  Too bad you're not looking forward to the 14th as well as the 15th. I'm looking forward to the 14th but not the 15th. Does offering to buy me things along the way constitute another bribe? Don't think you can

May 19

Enclosed is my senior picture so you know who to meet at the plane. See you the 15th.

Berkeley

4

"God, Berkeley, Europe!" Mitzi said as we put away the yogurt toppings at closing on Saturday night. "I just can't get over it. I can't believe you even considered not going."

Mitzi and I were both the beneficiaries of our mothers' unrealized dreams. I was named for the university my mother hadn't gotten to, and Mitzi's mother had wanted to dance in Hollywood musicals, the kind that lost popularity before she could get there. As a result, or maybe through our DNA, I'd aimed for college—though not specifically Berkeley—since the fifth grade, and Mitzi, college-bound, too, as a drama major, had been in every school theatrical production from junior high on.

"You know why I considered not going," I said.

"I know what you said, but I don't get the relevance." She ate a spoonful of carob chips before she poured the rest into a plastic bag. "A trip is a trip. Does it matter who you take it with? If I could get somebody to pay my way, I'd go anywhere."

Mitzi had a lioness spirit *and* a lioness heart. I always hoped some of it would rub off on me, but it hadn't yet. I liked to hear her talk, though. It gave me a feeling of vicarious daring. I took one last swipe at the counter and threw the towel into the laundry hamper.

"Maybe you and he'll become best friends," Mitzi said. "Maybe he was just waiting for you to grow up. Some men are like that, you know. They don't know how to act with little kids. They like them better when they're grown up. Then there's my father, who wants me *never* to grow up. The way I have to fight to get him to let me go out with even the most parentally acceptable guys. Not that they're much fun to be with. Not that I've been able to find anybody who would really give my father cause to worry. I swear, Berk, I think something's happening to today's men, something right up there with the rain forests disappearing and the hole in the ozone layer. Maybe they're even connected somehow. Men are just so, so out there, you know what I mean? And women are so *there*. No meeting ground, you know?"

"I've definitely noticed. Are you done? Let's get out of here."

"Right. I'm dying for some ice cream. I don't care how good for you yogurt is, I can't stand it. There's no way I'd work here except it's so easy to juggle my schedule around my rehearsals." Mitzi turned out the lights and locked the front door.

"It doesn't hurt that your mother owns the place."

"Well, yeah. That, too. Let's go to Ice Cream Dream. Katie told me there's a really cute guy working there."

"And you believed her? Somebody who goes out with Lawrence Carter?"

"Well, there's got to be *one*, somewhere, don't you think? One, just one, is all I ask, who's got my name secretly branded on his frontal lobe and when he sees me he'll immediately know. Mitzi, my angel! Where have you been?" She flung her arms wide and tipped her face up to the stars.

"All right," I said. "Let's go have a look at this man of your dreams."

Mitzi fished in her purse for the keys and unlocked the doors of her car. "Do you think optimism is wise or foolish?" she asked.

I knew the signs of somebody in a hurry to close up. I'd done it often enough myself—trying to get the counters wiped, the floor mopped, the trash cans emptied, everything done while there were still customers in the place, all the time praying, "Please don't let anybody else come in, please, please, please—especially not one minute before closing."

The boy behind the counter was doing all that and the look he gave us when we came through the door should have turned us to stone. There was no one else in the place.

"Are you sure you want ice cream?" I whispered to Mitzi.

"Ooo, look at him," Mitzi whispered back. "I'll have whatever takes the longest to eat."

"Remember how anxious we are to get out as soon as Yogurt City closes?" I asked her. "Remember how we hate it when someone comes in at the last minute? Remember how we don't care who it is, we just want them to leave?"

By now we were standing in front of the counter. Mitzi gave the boy—*Spike* was embroidered on the pocket of his shirt—one of her most theatrical smiles and said, "Do you have Butter Brickle?"

"Never heard of it," he said in a monotone, squeezing the rag in his hand.

"How about Cherry Ripple? Do you have that?"

"We have what's there. Why don't you look?" He turned back to washing the shake machine.

"Mitzi." I grabbed her arm and whispered in her ear. "Can't you tell your name isn't on his frontal lobe? He wants to push us out the door."

"Well, it's still three minutes to closing. I won't be hurried," she said stiffly. "What do you want?"

"Vanilla," I said. I couldn't help it. That's my favorite flavor. "One scoop. In a dish, please."

The boy had the ice cream ready almost before I'd finished speaking, and then he glared at Mitzi while I paid him.

"Oh, okay," she said. "I'll have one scoop of Pralines 'n' Cream, one scoop of Mint Chocolate Chip, and I'll have marshmallow sauce on the Pralines 'n' Cream and caramel on the Mint Chocolate Chip and just a little bit of whipped cream and a tiny sprinkle of nuts." She beamed at him. "Please."

The instant the hour hand on the wall clock touched eleven, Spike interrupted making Mitzi's concoction to lock the door and turn the sign to CLOSED.

"You know," Mitzi said to Spike, "anybody would think you were in a big hurry to get somewhere."

"Don't you ever want to get out of Yogurt City in a hurry?" he asked, handing her her dish and taking her money.

"How did you know I work at Yogurt City?" Mitzi asked, looking pleased.

"Because you're wearing a Yogurt City uniform," Spike and I said at the same time. Spike laughed and then I did, too. We looked at each other. Oh, my, my, my.

"Berkeley's an unusual name," Spike said, reading my name tag.

"So is Mitzi," Mitzi said, tapping her name tag   31

with her spoon. "My mother wanted to be an actress."

"My mother wanted to go to UC Berkeley," I said.

"You're lucky she didn't want to go to Harvey Mudd," Spike said.

I laughed and looked down into my dish of ice cream, feeling flustered and giddy. "You want to close up," I said. "We know how that is. We can finish our ice cream outside."

Mitzi shot me a stubborn look.

"No hurry," Spike said. "I can do my closing stuff while you eat." He cleaned out the cash register and put the money in the safe. "I'm trying to get to a party." He hesitated. "You want to come along?"

Mitzi looked at me and then made a grimace of pain. "I have to be home by midnight."

"Me, too," I said. "Thanks, anyway."

Spike shrugged. "Just thought I'd ask."

"We better go," I said. "Come on, Mitzi."

"Come in again," Spike said after us. "We're always open until eleven. I'd rather have ice cream than yogurt any day of the week."

"Me, too," Mitzi said, waving her spoon at him. "Bye. Sorry about the party."

Once we were outside, I said, "Would you really have gone to a party with somebody you know nothing about?"

"Come on, Berk. Nobody who looks as yummy as that could be dangerous."

"Ha. Remember Ted Bundy? Maybe a hundred

murders?" I threw my empty dish into a trash can in the parking lot. I heard what I was saying and I knew it was true, but I really couldn't believe anybody who looked as yummy as Spike could be dangerous either. Still, as usual, I leaned in the direction of rabbit-heartedness.

Mitzi propped herself against the fender of her car and kept eating her ice cream. "Where's your sense of adventure? Wasn't he a doll? And after he relaxed, he was nice, too."

"Mitzi, how do you know he was really going to a party? He could have taken you anywhere."

"He asked us both," Mitzi said, licking her spoon. "He'd have to be a gymnast."

"Mitzi! You know what I'm talking about."

"Yeah, yeah, I know. But being careful *all* the time takes so much of the fizz out of life. There's nothing like a little danger to make you feel wide-eyed and all there."

I sighed. She was probably right.

When Mitzi dropped me off at home, Lily and Grady were in the kitchen doing the Sunday paper's challenger crossword puzzle.

"Hi, Berkeley," Grady said. "I never can remember the word for extinct wild ox."

"Don't look at me," I said. "Can't you guys wait until tomorrow? There's something unseemly about doing the Sunday puzzle on Saturday."

"Berkeley, you sound like a fussbudget," Lily said. "Everything go okay at work?"

I felt like a fussbudget. "Yeah, fine," I said, taking a sip from Lily's teacup.

"I brought you an article," Grady said. "One of my better finds, I must say."

I read it aloud:

Antonio Gonzales of New York City won American Cyanamid's "biggest cockroach" contest at the Philadelphia Zoo last summer with a two-inch entry. At a similar contest in NYC earlier in the summer, five entries were disqualified when judges discovered that pieces of various cockroaches had been glued together to make larger ones.

I shook my head. "What some people will do with their time. It makes you wonder."

"Makes doing the Sunday crossword on Saturday look pretty tame, doesn't it?" Grady asked.

5

$\mathcal{S}$undays at Yogurt City were always slow until about three o'clock. At two, Mitzi was filing her nails and I was working on the challenger crossword. What *was* the word for extinct wild ox?

We both looked up when the bell on the door tinkled and in walked Spike.

"Well, hi," Mitzi said, putting down her nail file. "I thought you hated yogurt."

"Don't you have anything else?" he asked.

"At Yogurt City? Be serious. Well, we do have soft drinks." She smiled winsomely. In the senior play she had been the ingenue and she slipped back into that character occasionally.

"Okay. I'll have a Coke." He handed Mitzi some money. "Hi, Berkeley."

"Hi," I said, hoping I sounded more casual than I felt. "I don't suppose you know a four-letter word for extinct wild ox?"

"It's 'urus.' "

"What?"

"U-R-U-S."

"How in the world do you know that?"

"I used to do a lot of crossword puzzles. My ninth-grade English teacher thought it was good for our vocabularies. I've forgotten most of the weird clues, like rubber tree and small European apple and scene of Hannibal's defeat, but for some reason I remember urus."

How could this be a dangerous guy? How many serial killers knew the word for extinct wild ox?

He took his Coke from Mitzi and came to lean over the counter, turning the paper so he could see the puzzle, too.

"This one, 'mine in Savoie,' that's *à moi.*"

"What does that mean? I don't even understand the clue. A gold mine? A land mine? What's Savoie?"

"It's a place in France. Mine, meaning belonging to me, in French, is *à moi.*"

"Oh, yeah. I took two years of French, but it seems 36 to have mostly sieved right through my head."

"I'm trying to learn some." He lowered his voice as if he was going to tell me a secret. "I'm going to France this summer."

"No kidding," I said. "When?"

"Right after graduation. On a student tour. We're going to England and France for three weeks."

"What a coincidence. I'm going there, too. With my . . . father."

"Yeah? That *is* a coincidence. It would be something if we bumped into each other." He gave me a smile that could have sold a lot of toothpaste.

"Yeah; it would," I said. "Here, try your French skills on this one. 'Seine current separators.' Is that AC or DC?"

"It's *îles*. Islands. That's what's in the river Seine."

"Well, of course." I penciled it in. Not only did he have a great smile, he was smart. I was hoping he didn't think I was too dumb because of my denseness at crossword puzzles.

"Would it be, I mean, I wonder if you'd mind if I called you sometime," he said quickly. "We could talk about our trips."

I kept my eyes on the puzzle. The last thing I wanted to see was what was happening on Mitzi's face. "Sure." I wrote my phone number on the edge of the newspaper, tore it off, and handed it to him.

"Great," he said. "I've got to go to work now. I'll talk to you later." On the way out the door, he turned and said, "Oh, bye, Trixie."

37

"Mitzi!" she yelled at him. "Trixie," she sniffed when the door had closed. "Sounds like a performing poodle."

I pictured a dancing poodle with a bow on its head and Mitzi's face, and stifled a giggle.

"So you're giving your phone number to another Ted Bundy," she said. "I told you he was okay. Berk, I think you better get a look at that boy's frontal lobe. Oh, why is so much of life just uncontrollable chemistry?"

My personal chemistry did feel somewhat out of control. Was I about to get hit by that big wave?

Still, I was surprised when Spike actually called me that same night after I'd gotten home from Yogurt City. I was in the kitchen fixing myself a salad when the phone rang. I had a piece of carrot in my mouth and my hello was muffled.

"Berkeley? Is that you?"

"It's me. Who's this?"

"Spike Sullivan."

"I don't know any—oh, *Spike*. I didn't know your last name. Hi. I'm eating a carrot." I could feel my heart beating in my throat and hoped that, if he could hear it, he would think it had something to do with the carrot.

"It's probably really a cupcake and you're just embarrassed to say so."

"I am not. After looking at sweet stuff all day, I can 38 hardly wait to get home to vegetables and vinegar."

"I know what you mean." He sounded as if he was smiling. "My next job's going to be in a chili parlor."

We spent half an hour on the groundwork: where we went to school, how many pets and/or siblings we had, where we were born, what college we were going to next year. When I learned he was going to UCLA, too, I couldn't help thinking about fate and destiny. Then the information exchange narrowed to a purpose: do you see anybody special? Neither of us did. What hours do you work? Amazingly similar; he worked half an hour later than I did on Saturdays; on Sundays and Fridays we both got off at nine. Then the big one: he asked me if I was doing anything Friday after work. I told him he'd have to pick me up at home so Lily could meet him.

She wouldn't let me go out with anybody she hadn't met. She had also suggested it wouldn't hurt if I told my dates that she had a black belt in karate and was a student of voodoo curses. She didn't intend for me to end up married at seventeen, the way she had.

Before we hung up, I asked Spike what his real name was. "Spike sounds like a guard dog or a member of a motorcycle gang," I said.

"My brother started calling me that when I was a baby because my hair grew in all stiff and spiky."

I had a hard time imagining his thick straight hair being spiky. It wasn't so hard imagining what it would feel like in my fingers. I swallowed. "You haven't told me what your real name is."

He groaned. "Not until I know you better." 39

"That bad?" Well, he had to have *one* fault. "Is it Rumpelstiltskin?"

"Almost. I'll see you Friday." We hung up.

My blood felt carbonated. I called Mitzi.

"Oh, why does it always happen to somebody else?" she wailed. "Why don't *I* ever get the fateful encounter? It was *my* idea to go to Ice Cream Dream. Oh, I don't care. Take him. My destiny lies elsewhere, apparently. I'll become the famous star with the mysterious past. You'll be the ordinary person living happily ever after in the rose-covered cottage."

"Perhaps you're rushing things," I suggested.

"No, I'm not. I can feel these things. I must be allergic to romance. The very thought of it makes me want to . . . want to . . . makes me want to have some," she cried, while I laughed at her dramatics and hoped she wasn't jinxing me with her predictions.

Lily had a party to go to Friday night but she wasn't about to leave until after she'd met Spike. I was afraid nine-thirty seemed too late for a respectable date, but Lily just gave me a look and asked me what else I was supposed to do when I worked until nine.

By nine-thirty I'd showered and dressed and was debating whether I needed one more squirt of perfume, when the doorbell rang. I heard Lily's footsteps, the sound of the door opening, and Lily saying, "I'm Berkeley's mom. Come on in."

I brushed my hair, brushed it again, put on lipstick,

rubbed some off, daringly put on the extra squirt. I took a deep breath and went down the hall to the living room.

"Spike and I were comparing ice-cream-dipping careers," Lily said when I came through the door. "I'd forgotten about that callus you get on your thumb from the dipper. That's something you're saved from with the yogurt machine."

"Hi," Spike said, standing up.

"Hi," I said.

"Well," Lily said after a moment of silence while Spike and I looked at each other. "If you're ready to go, I'll go with you." At Spike's startled look, she laughed and said, "I mean at the same time. I'm going to a party. I only want to meet Berkeley's dates, not go on them."

Once in Spike's car, I said, "Okay, tell me your real name."

"Not yet," he said. "I have to be sure I can trust you not to spread it around. You have to pass all my security checks."

"Can it be odder than Berkeley? Worse than Mitzi?"

"I think Berkeley's a good name," he said. "But Mitzi—that one is almost as bad as mine."

"I know why Mitzi and I got our names. Why did you get yours?"

"My parents are name nuts. My dad's a linguistics professor and my mother writes romance novels. Her

41

characters all have names like January and Link and Fairfax."

"Dare I ask your brother's name?"

"He'd kill me if he knew I told you. Can you keep a secret? This is one of my security checks, by the way."

"I'll never tell, even under torture."

"Okay. It's Vachel. That's French for keeper of the cattle."

"My goodness. Berkeley's starting to seem quite tame. And is Vachel what you call him?"

"Are you kidding? He makes everybody call him Cowboy. Even my mother, who *loves* the name Vachel."

"Cowboy and Spike," I mused. "They sound like they should be in one of your mother's books."

"Well, actually, they are. They're hamsters that belong to January and Fairfax's little boy—his name is Thane. Fairfax was never sure Thane was really his son. You see, January had a tragic secret in her past."

"What was it?"

"I don't know. Probably that her name was really Edna."

I was sorry we were already at the theater, although holding hands with Spike in the dark for two hours turned out to be as good as talking to him, but in a different way.

After the movie, over hamburgers, Spike asked,
42 "Where's your dad?"

"L.A.," I said.

"Divorced?"

I nodded. "I haven't seen much of him. He left when I was a baby and has made himself scarce ever since."

"I thought you were going to Europe with him."

"I am, but I don't want to."

"Sounds like you have a tragic secret in *your* past."

"I don't know how tragic it is, but I've been pretty angry with him for a long time. Lily thinks this trip might change that. I can't see how, but she thinks he might have been transformed over the years, turned into somebody more interested in being a father. Even if he has, I'd say it's too late."

"He's made you a nice offer if he does want to make things better. Maybe you should give him a chance."

"Why should I? He hasn't given me anything."

He held up his hands. "Okay, fine. Do you know where you'll be in Europe, and when? Maybe we could get together, you know, if we happen to be in the same town at the same time. You might like to see a face from home if the trip's going the way you seem to think it will."

Seeing Spike in Europe seemed like a good idea no matter how the trip was going. "I could write him and ask. I'm not up to phoning. Writing gives me time to figure out how to say things."

"You don't have to. It was just a thought."

"No, it's okay. I want to."   43

Spike parked the car in front of my house. "Would you go out with me again tomorrow?" he asked.

"I don't finish work until ten-thirty."

"That's okay. I don't get off until eleven. You could come to my house. We could rent a movie, or do crossword puzzles. Or cook vegetables."

"Okay," I said, without giving a thought to the propriety of a date that began at eleven o'clock.

"Can you come by Ice Cream Dream when you're finished?"

"I'll have Mitzi drop me off."

We sat silently in the car for a minute. I looked down at my hands in my lap. Spike drummed his fingers on the steering wheel. Then he cleared his throat and got out of the car. My shoulders slumped with disappointment.

He walked me to the front door, where Madge sat hunched on the doormat. The porch light was burned out.

"Well, good night," I said. "I'll see you tomorrow." I took my key from my pocket and had just turned to put it in the lock when Spike leaned toward me. He grazed my forehead with his chin and, off-balance, stepped on Madge, who yowled and ran down the porch steps. The front door swung open and Lily stuck her head out.

"Oh, sorry," she said. "I heard Madge and thought something was after her."

44

"I was just coming in," I said, ducking my head. I could feel the blush rising all the way from my toes. "Good night, Spike."

"Good night," he muttered and shambled off to his car.

Lily closed the door. "Did I interrupt something?"

"Oh, I don't know," I said, flouncing into the living room and throwing myself on the couch. "Why is the porch light out? It made it look like I *wanted* him to kiss me."

"It did? I just forgot to replace it," Lily said, following me into the living room. *"Did* you want him to kiss you?"

"And then dumb Madge got in the way and he stepped on her," I said, avoiding her question. Of course I wanted him to kiss me. Why couldn't I have shown him I was interested in the idea? Would he ever try again? How could I let him know I wanted him to? I threw my head back on the sofa pillows. Romance was hell. Why Mitzi wanted some was beyond me.

I could see Lily was trying not to laugh about Madge. "Did you have a good time otherwise?" she asked.

I nodded. "I'm going out with him again tomorrow. After work."

"So now a late date is respectable?' she asked, smiling.

"Oh, okay, so that was silly. Maybe I was too—I wanted to start out—I mean, how did I know he'd be so—oh, never mind."

45

"So should I replace the porch light by tomorrow night?"

"Yes," I said emphatically. Then, "Well, maybe not." I gave her a sheepish look.

She patted my hand. "I remember," she said. "I used to like that part of a date, too."

I couldn't stand to think that she'd once felt about my father the way I was feeling about Spike.

6

May 27

I wonder if you could send me the itinerary for our trip. A friend of mine will be leaving the same day we are, going to England and France, and we were wondering if we might be in any of the same places at the same time.

Berkeley

The next night Spike and I ate vegetables and watched a movie on the VCR. Spike's parents tactfully went to bed right after we got there, but not before Mrs. Sullivan vowed to name one of her heroines Berkeley.

I was happy to discover that without the complications of Madge, Lily, and the porch light, Spike and I were able to make perfectly clear to each other what we wanted. I haven't a lot to compare him with, but I think it would be hard to find a better kisser than Spike Sullivan.

When he drove me home, we sat in the car looking at the darkened porch. "Tomorrow?" he asked. He looked at his watch. "I guess I mean today."

"I have to work. When are we going to study for finals?"

"We'll find time. How important is it, anyway? We've already been accepted to college. I have to know when I'm going to see you again."

I had trouble getting my breath. My rabbit heart was beating so hard it almost hurt. "Tomorrow, then, or today. Whatever."

"And the next day? And the next? Until we both leave for Europe? That's only eighteen days."

My lioness spoke. "Yes." He kissed me. "Now will you tell me your real name?" I whispered.

"You have to promise not to laugh."

"I promise."

"It's Crispin."

"Crispin." I tried out the sound of it. "I like it. It sounds like you."

"It's from the Latin. It means curly-haired."

"You're not." By now I knew what that thick straight hair felt like.

"Spike doesn't fit me either."

"What would you rather be called?"

"I think a number would be easier. Why don't you just call me Number One?"

June 1
Dear Berkeley,

I haven't a firm itinerary for us. I must be in London for a few days first, and then in Paris. Between those two stops we'll have several days on our own. Why don't you get your friend's itinerary and we'll try to meet up with her a time or two.

With love, Dad

The next eighteen days were a kind of delicious torment. Each one brought me closer to the dreaded trip with my father. Each one also brought me closer to Spike.

We spent every minute together that wasn't indisputably claimed by some other activity. Even sleep didn't seem more important than being with him. Of course, I had to listen to Mitzi go on about uncontrollable chemistry and karma and lucky stars and so on, especially when she found out Spike was going to UCLA, too. But she was right. How could I argue with her when my own stars felt so lucky and my own chemistry so uncontrolled? The rabbity part of me seemed in hibernation.

I packed for my trip in bare snatches of time between the other, more important parts of my life. I was probably forgetting lots of essential things, but I didn't care. Why should I spend a minute thinking about anything to do with my father when there were finals and graduation and parties and Spike to think about. Especially Spike.

One night, as I ran out the door to Spike, who was waiting in the car at the curb, Lily stopped me. "Berkeley, when are you going to get organized for this trip?"

"I'm organized enough," I said. "I'm not going to Mars."

"Do you have some idea that if you don't get ready in time you won't have to go?" she asked.

"Of course not. I know I'm stuck." But there was something to what she had said that resonated in me, and I knew I was still hoping for a way out. But how could I think about that now, when Spike was waiting. "I've got to go, Lily. Don't worry. I'll be ready."

"Pretty bracelet," Spike said, after he'd kissed me.

"Lily's friend Nell gave it to me for graduation. And Mom gave me this ring—" I waggled my finger in his face. "And Grady gave me stuff for my trip— a money belt and an inflatable pillow and a currency converter I'll never be able to figure out. But the best thing he gave me was a bunch of his funny articles. Like, you've had too much to drink if you can't easily pronounce 'truly' or 'rural' or 'biblical' or 'criticism.' "

"What else?"

I loved that he always wanted to know more, that he asked questions. How do you know somebody's interested in you unless they ask you questions? My father didn't do that. Never had.

"Oh, what else?" I said, trying to remember. "Well, did you know that turtles see in color? That Mary, Queen of Scots, loved billiards so much that when she was beheaded she was buried in the cloth ripped off her billiard table? That secretaries in a French law firm filed a complaint that the lawyers taped mirrors to their shoes so they could look up the women's dresses?"

Spike laughed. "I'd like to meet this Grady someday."

"He'll be at my graduation. So will Nell. They're taking time off to come with Lily, even if my father can't fit it into his schedule."

Spike took my hand. "I wish I could be there."

"You'll be at your own."

"I know. But I still wish I could be there. With your family."

I put my head on his shoulder. He understood so easily.

All through graduation Lily took rolls and rolls of pictures of me doing everything: walking, sitting, taking my diploma, throwing my mortarboard, blowing my nose. Having a photographer for a mother can be embarrassing, but I knew I'd never be sorry she took so many pictures of me with my friends. Especially with Mitzi.

"Mitzi," Lily said, "please stop crying. You don't want to look weepy in all the pictures, do you?"

"I can't help it," Mitzi said. "This is a very emotional time. The end of childhood. The beginning of real life, real responsibility, real—"

"Oh, Mitzi, you've got at least four years of college ahead of you," Lily said, laughing. "You can avoid responsibility for a while longer."

Mitzi perked up. "You think so? In that case . . ." and she turned a radiant smile in the direction of the camera, a smile that looked splendid in the finished prints, the tears in her eyes giving her a sparkle that made me look lackluster beside her.

When the picture-taking was finally finished, Mitzi said, "Now let the games begin. I know you have to go meet your dream man, Berk, so I'll see you at the Goldman twins' party later, right?"

"I'm not sure when. We have his parties to go to as well as mine, so we'll be moving fast. And that means I better get going."

"You want me to turn in your cap and gown for you?" she asked. "You probably don't want to wear them to the parties."

That's how distracted I was; I'd forgotten what I was wearing. I pulled my gown off. "It helps with the figure flaws, but it sure doesn't have much style," I said, hanging it over Mitzi's outstretched arm and putting my mortarboard on top of it.

"You don't have any figure flaws," she said. "Anyway, we have to turn them in right now. The robes, not the figure flaws, though don't I wish. I love your new dress, Berk. You look fabulous."

"Thanks." I hugged her. "And thanks for being my friend for so long. I couldn't have grown up without you."

Mitzi dropped my cap and gown and hugged me back hard. "Stop, or you'll make me cry again."

Lily took another picture.

As soon as Mitzi and I let go of each other, Nell moved in for a hug. "Bop till you drop tonight, honey. And have a great trip."

"Yes on the bopping," I told her. "I doubt it on the trip."

"Do I get one of those, too?" Grady asked.

I hugged him, too. "Thank you for the travel gear, Grady. I can dazzle other tourists with my little-known fact about Mary, Queen of Scots."

"Enjoy yourself," he said. "And watch out for zee Frenchmen wiz zee leetle meerors on zere shoos."

I laughed and grabbed Lily's hand, dragging her toward the parking lot while she called her goodbyes over her shoulder.

When we pulled into the driveway, Spike was just arriving at the curb. Lily let the car idle as she said to me, "This will be the first Wednesday night we haven't shoveled out the house together in a long time. I guess I'd better get used to it."

"Oh, Lily," I said. I unfastened my seat belt and

53

leaned awkwardly across the gearshift to hug her. "Thank you for the beautiful ring and . . . and for everything. For just being my mom."

Lily sniffed in my ear. "It was my pleasure," she said.

"It's not over," I said. "There'll be more pleasures."

"I know," she said, still holding on to me. "But it's going to be different now. There's Spike and your trip and college. You aren't all mine anymore."

"Do you want that?" I asked, knowing I had to say something to keep myself from crying. "Do you want me to still be hanging around when I'm forty, nagging you to play with me every night when you get home from work?"

"God forbid," she said, with a watery chuckle. She let me go. "Spike's waiting. Have fun. When will I see you again?"

"In time to go to the airport tomorrow. Don't worry, I'll be ready." I kissed her and ran across the lawn to Spike.

More hugging and kissing when I got into the car. I could get used to days like this. When he let me go, he said, "So, do you feel ready for the cold, cruel world now?"

"No. I refuse to go."

"Okay. I have an idea. Why don't we jaunt around Europe for a while and then hide out in the womb of

54   higher education for a few more years?"

"Great idea."

He kissed me again. "A girl after my own heart." His voice softened. "A girl who's got my heart." He handed me a small box. "Happy graduation."

"Oh, Spike. Oh, Spike." I couldn't seem to say anything else as I tore the paper off. In the box was a tiny gold bee on a thin gold chain.

"Bee for Berkeley," Spike said.

"I love it. Help me put it on." After he'd fastened it around my neck, I handed him his gift. "Something you can use in your pursuit of higher education—to keep it from getting away from you." I'd gotten him a paperweight in the shape of a gilded railroad spike. I thought it was very clever of me.

So did he. "Perfect," he said.

"I know," I said modestly.

Laughing, we drove off to our first party.

It was false dawn when Spike brought me home. We were both wired on that edgy combination of exhaustion and stimulation and we were still unwilling to say good night. How could we when we didn't know when we'd see each other again and an hour's separation already felt like too much.

"We'll get together in Europe, I know we will," he said. "Your dad sounds willing to do that."

"He thinks you're a girlfriend, remember? He may not be so willing when he finds out otherwise."

"Why not?"

"How should I know? I don't know anything about him."

"Then be optimistic." I thought of Mitzi asking me if I thought being optimistic was wise or foolish. I still didn't know. Spike played with my fingers. "I'm going to miss you."

"Me, too," I said. "Does it worry you at all how fast this has happened?"

"Worry me? No. I think it's terrific. It's a myth that guys don't want to be involved with somebody. I think it's what every person wants, excluding a few nuts and hermits. Anything else is just too lonely."

"But you're not alone. You have lots of friends."

"And they're great. I'm glad I have them. But having somebody special, somebody you feel differently about than you do about anyone else, and she feels the same about you—that's the best. Don't you think so?"

"Well, sure, but it's still scary. I worry about getting hurt."

"But I would never hurt you. Not on purpose."

"What about accidentally?" Evidently my rabbit heart had awakened.

"Berkeley, an accident's an accident. Don't be afraid. Sure, we're taking a risk. That's what makes this exciting."

"Risk has never been in my top ten things. I want a guarantee that we'll work out, that no one will be

56   hurt."

"Well, sure, I'd like that, too. But forget it. Can't you just enjoy what's happening with us? I am."

"I want to understand it better. I don't like feeling so mystified about why."

"Why? Well, there's certainly chemistry, like Mitzi's always saying."

"No kidding," I said, and rubbed his hand against my cheek. "But what else? What makes people get along or not?"

"I suppose it has to do with what you get from someone and what you want to give them. You make me laugh and you're the best listener I've ever known and you have interesting things on your mind. I like that you're thoughtful, even if it makes you a little bit of a worrier. You give me things I need."

Oh, yes, that was it. That was why I loved the people I did. They gave me what I needed. Something Parker Stanton had never done.

"And you do to me," I said. "You ask good questions—I've always been a sucker for a good question-asker."

"I have one for you now. Are you sure you have to go in? Can't we go get some breakfast?"

"Sure," I said. "I can't think of a single reason why not."

By the time I got home, there was barely time to shower and change, forget about sleeping. I threw a few last things into my suitcase and crossed my fingers 57 that I had what I needed, because I didn't want to think about it. I couldn't have been in worse shape to meet my father: tired almost to the point of delirium, and emotionally overloaded. I'd deliberately done nothing to ensure that I would be ready, in any way, for this reunion.

7

"Can I ask one thing?" Lily said on the way to the airport.

"What?" I knew I sounded sullen, but I was stupid with fatigue and caught between blaming Lily for what I now thought of as making me go, and wanting to cling to her and cry, "Let me stay home," just the way I'd done before day camp when I was seven.

"Send me a postcard every day. Just so I'll have a record of where you've been. I'll save them for you so you can remember your trip. Only a few lines. Could you do that?" Lily snapped the rubber band on her wrist.

I knew this was hard for Lily, too, and I knew what she was really asking for. But at that moment it seemed too demanding, too much of a chore: buying cards, finding stamps, mailboxes, thinking what to write. Why did everything have to be so difficult?

"Oh, okay," I said grudgingly. My eyes burned. "Don't park. I'll get out at the curb."

"Don't you want me to wait with you until you board?"

"No. It's too awkward to keep making farewell conversation. I just want to get this over with."

Lily opened her mouth to say something, but closed it again. Then she said, "All right." She pulled into a ten-minute unloading zone and got out to unlock the trunk.

I heaved my luggage from the trunk to the sidewalk, a suitcase and a carry-on bag. They both seemed ridiculously heavy, considering the fact that I felt I'd hardly packed anything.

"I'll miss you," Lily said. "I hope it's all right."

"To miss me?"

"No, silly. The trip."

"Yeah. Me, too." This was a fine time for Lily to worry about the trip being all right.

"Well, goodbye, honey." Lily hugged me quickly and got back into the car.

I picked up my bags and marched into the terminal. Terminal, I thought. How ominous.

I fell asleep as soon as I fastened my seat belt, and woke, disoriented and panicky, at the end of the forty-five-minute flight.

What if he wasn't there? What if he was there but didn't recognize me without the white gauze around my shoulders and the theatrical makeup of my senior picture? The last time I'd seen him, I'd been fourteen, with braces on my teeth and bad skin. The last time I'd talked to him on the phone—when *had* that been? —I hadn't been able to think of anything to say. What if he wanted to pretend everything was fine between us? My head hurt and my breath seemed stuck in my chest.

I was so groggy and disorganized I was the last one off the plane and had to walk down a long corridor before I came to the place where passengers could be met. There was a throng of people in my way and I was having trouble remembering what my father looked like. Dark hair was all I could think of. Lily always said how handsome he was, but the old photos she had of him looked like they came from Prehistoric High School. Why hadn't he sent *me* a picture?

A hand fell on my arm and a deep voice said in my ear, "Berkeley?"

I turned and took a good look. Lily was right; he was one of the handsomest men I'd ever seen. I don't know why I'd forgotten that. Or ignored it, wanting to remember him as some sort of ogre. And his eyes were exactly the same as mine—the part of myself that I'd   61 always considered my best feature. That shock of recognition almost buckled my knees, and he seemed to sense it before I did, because his hand tightened on my arm until it seemed to be the only thing holding me up.

"Hi," I breathed, feeling weak and foolish.

"You're prettier than your picture," he said, still holding my arm.

"I'm sorry," I said irrelevantly. "I've been up all night." I didn't want to be nice to him. I wanted him to have to earn that, to earn it in spades.

"I was afraid you'd missed the plane."

"No," I said, making myself remember the birthday cards signed by someone else, the purple satin gloves.

"Wow," he said. "This is, it's, well, I don't know what to call it. Come on, let's get out of this mess. Have you got checked baggage?"

"No," I said, puzzled. "It's gray."

He smiled and several women passing us turned back to admire the sight. "I mean, did you check any baggage through, or did you carry it all on?"

"Oh," I said, feeling like an idiot. "I checked one bag."

He still held me by the arm, steering me through the crowds. "Was it a good flight?"

"I guess so. We didn't crash. I slept the whole way."

62   "You must have had a busy day yesterday. I'm

sorry I couldn't be there." He stopped in an unoccupied departure lounge and finally released my arm. He stood facing me. "We have the same eyes," he said. "I hadn't noticed that before."

There was a lot about me he hadn't noticed before. And while our eyes may have *looked* the same, they didn't *see* the same.

"Wow," he said again, sounding as if he'd reverted to the boy he'd been when he and Lily had conceived me. "Could I—that is, would you mind if I hugged you?"

I shrugged. Really, I'd expected him to do that when I first got off the plane, one of those L.A. kind of hugs that perfect strangers give each other. I was surprised he'd asked for my permission.

Carefully, he put his arms around me and hugged me to him. I submitted, but refused to hug him back. He smelled expensive and somehow confident, and the material of his sport coat scratched against my cheek. He started to release me and then hugged me close again. I felt his chest lift with a sudden indrawn breath.

I endured this Hollywood welcome until he let me go and stepped back, blinking and half laughing. "It's been a long time between hugs," he said.

And whose fault is that, I wanted to ask him.

"Well," he said, "we should retrieve your bag and get over to British Airways. Let me take your carry-on." He removed it from my shoulder and, holding it in one hand, took me by the arm again with his other hand and guided me along to the baggage claim. I felt as if I'd been taken prisoner.

We stood in the crowd by the baggage carousel, jostled together, our shoulders bumping. I took a step away from him, wondering if he noticed.

"So," he said brightly, "how's it feel to be all graduated?"

"I can't tell yet. I liked high school. Change isn't my favorite thing."

"Well, we'll have to fix that. Change is invigorating, cleans out the cobwebs. Keeps you on the edge."

"I don't like being on the edge."

"That's because you don't know what it's like," he insisted.

"I'm not interested in seeing what it's like." My head pounded.

"Well," he said heartily, "we'll have time to discuss that. And how is . . . Lily?"

"She's great. She's fantastic. She has a fabulous job and lots of friends. She gave me this ring for graduation." I thrust my hand out to him, the opal in my ring catching the light and looking as if atoms were fissioning inside the stone. "It's my birthstone."

"Is that right? I've heard opals are unlucky. But you're probably not superstitious."

"They're not unlucky if they're your birthstone. Then they're lucky." I felt like adding, *nanny nanny boo boo, so there.*

"Opals are September's birthstone?" he said. "I didn't know that. The only one I know is April. That's diamonds. Paula—my wife—her birthday is in April and she made sure I knew that."

"My birthday's in October."

"Of course," he said. "I always get those fall months mixed up. Of course it's in October. The seventeenth, right?"

"Right," I said, though I wished he'd been wrong. Why should he know his wife's birthstone and not mine?

He grabbed the bag I indicated from the carousel and we left the baggage area. "Paula's over at British Airways."

I looked at him. So?

He exhaled. "She's watching the carry-on stuff. I wanted to meet you by myself."

We stepped onto a moving sidewalk.

"She's anxious to get to know you," he said.

I didn't believe that for a minute. "We've only got two hours."

"Two—oh, until takeoff. Yes, that's right." He lapsed into silence for the rest of the long walk, for which I was grateful.

My father shepherded me through baggage check-in, passport control, and security. I wasn't too sleepy to notice that he kept my ticket. I would have preferred to hold on to it myself.

When we reached the British Airways waiting area, it was crowded. I scanned the faces to see if I could guess which one was my father's wife. I narrowed it down to either a tall, elegant woman with black hair smoothed back into a bun, exposing large gold earrings, or a petite blonde in a red velour designer sweat suit. She looked as if she could have been a cheerleader at some time in her past. When I noticed that the tall woman was accompanied by a girl of fourteen or so, I went with the blonde.

"Do you know why we have to be here so early?" I asked. Two hours of making conversation with him and his wife before I could even get on the plane seemed more than I could handle in my current state of exhaustion and hard feelings. Maybe the blond cheerleader would do all the talking.

"Lots of people to get through security and check-in and so on. Now I want you to meet my wife," he said. I started in the direction of the woman in red. "Over here," he said, pointing at the tall black-haired woman.

Up close, she was even more intimidatingly elegant, in her severe black linen pants outfit, than I'd thought when I'd first noticed her.

"Berkeley," my father said, "this is Paula, my wife."

Paula put out a slim, immaculately manicured hand with a wide, diamond-studded ring on her pinkie. I wondered if it had been a birthday present. She took my hand in her cool one and murmured, "Hello, Berkeley. I've been so looking forward to meeting you. And I'd like you to meet *my* daughter, Shelby." She put her hand on the shoulder of the girl I'd noticed before.

Shelby was dressed in black, too, but with none of her mother's style. Her outfit consisted of a loose black T-shirt, tight black jeans, and black boots with pointed, silver-trimmed toes. Her dishwater-blond hair was loose and shaggy around her closed and sulky face.

My own face probably looked about the same way. Good old Dad hadn't thought to mention to me that I had a stepsister. He'd barely remembered to tell me I had a step*mother*.

"Hi," I said to Shelby.

She grunted without looking at me and sat down, staring at the floor between her feet. Great. She hated me on sight.

"Did you two have any trouble finding each other?" Paula asked, seating us in the chairs she'd saved and beginning almost two hours of polite and inconsequential conversation. I had to admire how wonderful she was at it, keeping words flowing smoothly back and forth, asking questions which didn't require much thought to answer, or call for any revelations too personal. Even my father seemed lulled by Paula's masterful social skills. Shelby apparently hadn't acquired any of them, as she continued to contemplate

67

the floor and to keep her own silent counsel, something I wished I could join her at.

What were good old Dad and I to do for the rest of the trip without Paula to fill the spaces between us with her superficial fribble?

Finally, finally, our flight was called. I stood and slung my carry-on bag over my shoulder. I could hardly wait to close my eyes and sleep for the whole twelve hours to London.

"Thank you for coming to see us off," I said to Paula, wishing Lily were there to appreciate my ability to be courteous under the circumstances.

"See you off?" Turning to my father, Paula said, "Ace, do you mean you didn't tell her?"

Ace? Since when had he become Ace? And didn't tell me what? I glared in his direction, all my distrust and suspicion receptors on full alert.

He threw me an abashed look and turned to Paula. "I tried, but I . . . I never managed to."

"Tell me what?" I asked. If he'd been making any attempt to tell me something, I'd sure missed it.

He put his hands in his pockets, still looking at Paula. She shook her head. He turned back to me. "Paula and Shelby are going, too. With us. To Europe."

I could only stare at him. This was so ludicrous I would have laughed if I hadn't felt so betrayed. Of course they were going with us. We had all gone through the security check, but I had been too groggy to think about it. And now a trip I didn't want to go on with a person I didn't want to be with had just acquired two more reasons not to go.

My father took his hands from his pockets and held them out to me, his palms up. "I apologize, Berkeley. Really. I just didn't know how to tell you. I wanted you to come and I didn't want anything to spook you off."

I longed to run, to find a San Diego–bound plane and go home, to forget this entire ridiculous idea and this man I didn't want to be related to. "You deceived me," I said, and hardly recognized my own voice, furious and quavering.

"Not intentionally." He grabbed for my hands, which I clenched into fists in his grasp. He held them so tightly I couldn't pull away from him. "I meant to tell you. I'm sorry. I so much wanted you to come. It can still be a wonderful trip. Now you can get acquainted with Paula, too. And with your new sister."

Shelby's head came up at that. "Sister!" she said, looking at me with distaste.

"Oh, Ace," Paula said softly.

"I want to go home," I said, not caring if only my luggage went on to London; actually preferring it that way. "Give me my ticket. I'll exchange it for one to San Diego and send you the change."

"Please don't, Berkeley," he begged.

Boarding passengers swirled around us, pretending not to be curious about the drama occurring in their

69

midst. I wanted to denounce him to all of them, to tell them what he'd done to me, not just today but through all seventeen of the years he'd neglected and disappointed and enraged me.

"Please don't," he said again. "We've waited so long for this."

"I wasn't waiting," I said, managing to snatch one fist from his hand. "And why *was* it so long? Why *haven't* we done this before?"

"Oh, Berkeley, not now. Come with me. Give me a chance to tell you."

Shelby made a derisive sound in her throat and Paula gave her a look to rival Lily's Eye of Doom. Because Shelby was staring at the floor again, the look missed her.

"I don't need a father," I said spitefully. "I never have."

He hesitated and then said, "I need my daughter. Please come."

I trembled with emotion and fatigue. My brain seemed to have stopped working entirely. My father kept talking, but I'd quit listening after I heard "I need my daughter." The liar! The smooth-talking, manipulating—how did he know those were the words I'd always ached to hear? Had waited for on every birthday, every Christmas, through every visit with him, through every phone call.

But what if he wasn't lying? What if he had finally changed?

Why should I trust him? Why should I believe him?

"Berkeley," he said, "it's final boarding. Please come."

What if he wasn't lying?

I pivoted away from him and marched to the boarding gate.

ily was right about my father liking fancy things. We were flying first class. Before we could even sit down, the flight attendant was there, all over us with drinks and newspapers, pillows and eyeshades and hand lotion. I was too unsettled, too worried that I'd been railroaded, to enjoy the luxury.

"I want the window," Shelby said to me. "Do you have a problem with that?"

Of all the things I had problems with, that was way down on the list. "No," I told her. I'd be glad to sit anywhere as long as it wasn't beside my father.

Shelby dropped into the seat, pulled on her eye-shade, and turned her face to the window.

I was glad Ace—Ace!—and Paula were sitting behind us. I didn't want to have to look at him, even at the back of his head, for the whole flight.

I was fastening my seat belt when he appeared beside me. "All settled, girls?" he asked.

Shelby ignored him. I nodded.

"Nice plane, huh?" he said, sounding as if he'd built it himself.

I nodded again.

"You comfortable? Need a pillow? A blanket? Something to read?"

"Everything's fine," I said, which was hardly the truth.

"You can't beat first class for a long trip," he said just as the attendant suggested he take his seat for takeoff.

As we taxied down the runway, I thought of Spike, excited, full of French phrases, unencumbered by any baggage from the past, anticipating his own flight leaving that afternoon, good time practically guaranteed. I wished I'd been nicer to Lily on the way to the airport. I wished I'd sent her a postcard before we'd even taken off.

Still blinkered by her eyeshade, Shelby pushed her seat into a reclining position, pulled a blanket up around her shoulders, and arranged herself for sleep.

As soon as he could be, my father was out of his seat

again, squatting in the aisle to talk to me. "Okay, Berkeley, here's the best way to beat jet lag. London's eight hours ahead of us, so you turn your watch to London time and start operating as if it's really seven in the evening. You'll be amazed at how much it helps. So much of anything is attitude."

This was the wrong time to be talking to me about attitude. Besides, I was pretty sure jet lag had more to do with a body's natural rhythms than with its attitude. No matter what my father thought, not everything could be accomplished through sheer will.

But that didn't stop him. "Actually," he said, "the fact that you've been up all night is a good thing. You shouldn't have any trouble sleeping on the plane, and when we arrive in London, it'll be morning and you'll be all set."

He thought he was so smart. Even though I was so exhausted I felt like crying, I couldn't sleep for more than twenty minutes at a time without being awakened by something: the serving of a meal, or the start of a movie, or Shelby bumping past my legs as she got out of her seat, or the captain making some announcement, or just the ceaseless throbbing drone of the plane's engines. This pattern of blank sleep and startled wakefulness gave the trip an interminable, surrealistic quality that made me feel sick to my stomach. He'd probably say I just had a bad attitude.

74   I was too queasy to eat breakfast, though my father

had seconds on everything. Shelby slept through the meal, or pretended to. Paula looked as exquisitely groomed as she had however many hours ago it was that we had begun this nightmare trip, and I felt like I'd been dragged through a hedge backward.

"Really, Berkeley, you should eat," my father kept saying. "It's breakfast time." But my body knew it wasn't morning, no matter what Ace said. The poor thing didn't know what time it was, but no way could it be convinced this was morning.

Even when we began the landing pattern, he wouldn't let me alone. He leaned as far forward as his seat belt would allow, to say in my ear, "Look, Berkeley. Look how green England is. How beautiful, this sceptered isle."

I didn't know what a sceptered isle was and I didn't care.

Suddenly Shelby sat up, took off her eyeshade, which she threw to the floor, and ran her fingers through her hair, to no discernible effect. When the wheels hit the runway, she muttered to herself, "Beat the odds again."

Stumbling and sick, I trailed my father and Paula through the airport formalities—passports, baggage claim, customs—while Shelby, who apparently was pretending she didn't know any of us, followed even farther behind. I almost ran into Paula when she stopped without my noticing it.

"You stay here, my darlings," my father said, 75

"while I go change some money and see about the car."

Don't you dare call me your darling, I thought as I fell into a seat and put my head down on my knees.

"Can I do anything to help?" Paula asked, sitting next to me.

I shook my head, rolling it across my knees. "I just need some sleep."

"I know you do," she said. "These long flights are hell."

I looked up at her. "What about pretending it's morning?"

She quirked up one corner of her mouth and one eyebrow. "It's not morning," she said. "In a few days we'll think so, but not yet."

My father's voice cut through my half-doze. "The car's here and I've gained a lot of pounds. Get it, Berkeley? Pounds are English money, don't you know, as they say here. Well, let's get going."

I wanted to pound *him*.

I fell asleep in the car, which was a shame, because it was a limousine driven by a uniformed driver and I'd never been in a limo before. I woke with a jerk when the car stopped in front of our hotel. Ace said it was a restored Edwardian town house in the Mayfair district. I didn't care what it was as long as it had a bed.

The bellhops did everything but carry us from the car to the lobby, and the hotel manager rode with us in the brass cage of an elevator up to our suite. It was clear my father had stayed here before. And that he enjoyed the fuss.

I'd never seen such a hotel suite before except in a TV miniseries. There were fresh flowers and chilled champagne; Swiss chocolates and cheeses and fruit so perfect I thought at first it was wax; a fireplace and a fax machine. I gawked like a hayseed while Paula and my father moved around inspecting things and Shelby flung herself down on the sofa.

Apparently, everything met their satisfaction. My father tipped the bellhops with several unfamiliar bills —he was already losing some of his pounds, yuk, yuk—and poured four glasses of champagne, which he handed around.

"To us and London," he said, raising his glass and drinking it down in one gulp. I couldn't. My stomach was still too unhappy. But Shelby tossed hers off as my father had. Paula gave her a look, but didn't say anything, while she sipped daintily at her champagne.

"Okay, here's the plan," my father said. "We'll unpack, freshen up, and then take a walk. If you're hungry, have some of that." He gestured to the fruit and cheese basket. "I want you ladies to get the layout of the neighborhood, so while I'm off conducting business, you'll know where you are."

Shelby smirked at the word "ladies."

"Then," he continued, ignoring Shelby, "we'll

have tea somewhere and go to bed early. Tomorrow we'll all be in splendid shape."

"I don't feel like sightseeing," I said. "I need some sleep *now*."

"That would be a big mistake," he said. "If you sleep now, you'll feel jet-lagged forever. Ah, London, history on top of history. One of the great cities of the world. Let me show it to you."

An hour later he was at the door, holding it open as Paula and Shelby and I preceded him out. I didn't know who to be madder at, him or myself for so meekly doing what I didn't want to do. It was small comfort that Shelby looked as sullen as I felt. I would have given some pounds of my own to know what Paula said to her in the few minutes behind the closed door of Shelby's and my bedroom that got her to go with us. I was pretty sure that hadn't been Shelby's original plan.

The walk we took could have been fun if I'd been with Mitzi or Spike or Lily, no matter how tired I was. There was a lot to see, and any one of them would have teased me and coaxed me and cajoled me into seeing it, in spite of myself. Only with those closest to you can you be your whiniest, your realest self. Somehow, with strangers, you have to be on better behavior. At least I did. Shelby didn't seem to care.

Ace led us around, calling out sightseeing tips

which I didn't hear because of the roar of the traffic

and my own disinterest. When I thought I could go no farther, that I would have to lie down on the street and go to sleep, we turned into the Dorchester Hotel, where I fell into a chair at a tea table.

By now I was famished. Mercifully, tea turned out to be a lot more than that—sandwiches and pastries and scones with clotted cream, which sounded disgusting but tasted divine. Shelby pounced on the food with total concentration. She must have been as hungry as I was, but I had the feeling that she'd have starved before she'd have said so.

When we finally got back to our hotel, everyone scattered as if we'd had all we could stand of each other. I knew I had. Paula went to run a bath, Ace sat before the fire with the *International Herald Tribune*, and Shelby threw herself on her bed in our room without even removing her boots and seemed to fall instantly to sleep.

I had a couple of chores to take care of before I could do the same.

I stood before my father, hidden behind his newspaper, and asked, "Can I change some traveler's checks in the hotel? I want to buy some postcards."

He put down the paper and took out his wallet, removing several notes, which he handed me. He considered for a moment and then handed me a few more bills. "This should be enough for a while," he said. "Just ask me when you need more."

"I have my own traveler's checks," I said. 79

"This trip is my gift to you," he said. "You can ask me for whatever you need."

Well, he owed me. And as long as I was letting him pay for my hotel, food, and plane ride, it seemed silly not to take the walking-around money.

I bought postcards and stamps at the shop in the lobby. When I was paying for them, I showed the clerk all the money my father had given me and asked her, "How much is this in American dollars, do you know? What would it buy? A fancy meal, a car, what?"

"Cor," the girl said, her eyes widening. "Not a car, but a nice few days on holiday, or the lovely big color telly I've been saving up for. Wait, let me see." She made a calculation with her currency-converting computer. I had left mine at home, figuring I'd never learn to use it, and now I wished I'd brought it. If she could use one, so could I. When she told me how much I had in American, my eyes widened, too. I'd have to serve a lot of yogurt to earn that much.

I sat in one of the lobby's overstuffed armchairs to write my postcards.

June 16
Dear Mitzi,
    You would swoon to see some of the outfits walking around on the streets here. I wish you were with me.

                                               Berkeley

June 16
Dear Lily,

I almost wrote Dear Mom. Parker's new wife and stepdaughter came with us and I didn't know they were going to until we were nearly on the plane. Can you guess if I'm having a good time?

Berkeley

I left the postcards at the desk to be mailed and went back up to the suite. My father was still reading the paper.

"Get what you wanted?" he asked.

"Where are Paula and Shelby?" I asked.

"Shelby's still asleep, and Paula's still in the bath. There's nothing like these big deep English tubs. You can practically live in them."

I was almost past being tired and way past caring if I offended him. I needed to get some questions answered.

"How long have you and Paula been married?" I asked.

He folded the newspaper and dropped it on the floor. "Almost six months. I should have let you know, I realize that, but the time has gone by so fast. Her first husband died about a year and a half ago. I knew him slightly, and I'd met her at parties. She's beautiful, isn't she?"

"Yes," I agreed, even though I held a warmer, messier, livelier idea of true beauty. But by a purely   81 aesthetic standard, Paula was certainly beautiful. It didn't escape me how he glossed over the fact that he hadn't let me know when they got married.

"Did she have anything to do with you inviting me on this trip?" For all Paula's expertise at the inconsequential, I'd had a glimpse in the airport of a person who seemed to have a firm grasp of reality, and I was still looking for the reason for this invitation.

"Not directly, no," he said. "But when I suggested it, she encouraged me. Her father died when she was a little girl, and now the same thing's happened to her daughter. She thinks fathers are important to daughters." He had the grace to look embarrassed. "What do you think?"

"I have no experience in that department," I said. "I haven't seen enough of you to know." My voice broke operatically and I was afraid I was going to cry, but I wasn't going to stop now. I didn't want him to believe that the way he had treated me was okay with me.

He leaned toward me and put his hand on my arm. It was so unexpected I almost jumped. "Well, now I have two daughters and I want to be a good father to them both."

I stood up so fast I got dizzy, and the tears that had been threatening retreated. With stinging, embarrassing jealousy, I realized I resented being lumped in with Shelby. I was his *real* daughter and if anybody deserved special consideration at this turning point in his life it was me, not her. He might have thought he'd turned over a new leaf, but he and I weren't even reading the same book.

"What's wrong?" he asked, looking up at me. "I thought you'd be pleased. Things can be different for us now."

"You're way too late," I said. My spine felt as if it were made of ice. "I'm going to bed. I have jet lag whether I should or not."

He stood up and held his hand out to me. "But what . . . ?"

I turned my back on him and went into the bedroom, where Shelby lay, fully dressed and snoring, on her still made-up bed.

The only comfort I found, before I plummeted into sleep, was knowing that Spike was somewhere in this same city and that I could put money on him to remember, even if I were to wake him from a luscious dream, when my birthday was.

9

Paula woke Shelby and me the next morning. As far as I could tell, Shelby hadn't moved since the afternoon before. She still lay on her back, fully clothed, on top of the covers.

"Up, girls, up," Paula said cheerily. "Breakfast's on its way. Your father has to go to a meeting and he wants to see you before he goes."

"He's not my father," Shelby said.

I wished I could deny he was mine, too.

Shelby was in and out of the bathroom in five minutes and went straight into the sitting room without changing any of her clothes. I couldn't have been that fast even if I could think of a good reason why I should be. By the time I'd showered and dressed, breakfast was laid out on a table by the fireplace and the others were already eating.

My father stood when I entered the room, and pulled out a chair for me next to him. He was immaculately groomed and expensively dressed and looked like a million in any currency. "Good morning, Berkeley," he said. "I hope you'll forgive me for not waiting, but I have a meeting to get to. Did you sleep well?"

"Yes, fine." I sat down without looking him in the face.

"I ordered the works," he said. "The English may have their failings in the culinary department, but they do know how to do breakfast." He began lifting silver covers, naming the different dishes he uncovered: eggs, bacon, sausages, mushrooms and tomatoes, fried bread, kippers, porridge, stewed fruit. "I'm not sure what this is—deviled kidneys, I think," he said as he lifted the last cover.

"Gross," Shelby said, which was just what I was thinking. "So are kippers and stewed fruit and squishy tomatoes and fatty sausages and limp greasy bacon."

Paula gave her another of those looks which would have impaled her if Shelby ever met her mother's eyes.

85

"Just toast," I said, my stomach rebelling at Shelby's descriptions. I'd have given anything for a big glass of California orange juice, a slice of Health-Nut bread, and a cat in my lap.

My father took a final swallow of coffee, patted his mouth with a napkin, and said, "My car's waiting. We'll do something special for dinner. Goodbye, my beautiful women." He dropped a kiss on each of our heads as Paula smiled, Shelby tried to dodge him, and I, taken by resentment again as he consolidated us all into one, a harem at his convenience, sat like a stone. Apparently oblivious to our reactions, he grabbed his briefcase and an umbrella and left.

"I'm going to be doing the antique shops today," Paula said. "We need a lot of things for the new house. Would you girls like to come with me?"

"No," Shelby said. "And don't buy anything for my room. I want to keep my same old furniture."

"But it's so—" Paula began.

"I mean it," Shelby said. "I don't want anything new."

Paula sighed. "Well, maybe you girls would like to go to Madame Tussaud's. Or the Tower of London. You can see the Crown Jewels there."

"I'd rather see Traitors' Gate, or Tower Green, where they used to behead people. Or the Bloody Tower."

I almost laughed. Shelby was rebellious with style. Paula's lips compressed for an instant before she said, "Well, if that's what you want to see. It's very historic, I'm sure. But I'd appreciate it if you two would stay together. London is a big and strange city and neither of you knows her way around."

"I do so," Shelby said. "When we were here with Daddy, he showed me everything on the map and explained how the Underground works."

"Shelby, that was five years ago. You were only nine then. You can't possibly remember."

"Yes, I do," she said darkly. "I remember everything Daddy and I did together. Everything."

Paula sat perfectly still for a moment and then rose. "All right, Shelby. Whatever you say. But you and Berkeley must stay together. Is that understood?"

Shelby looked down at her breakfast plate in what could have been a nod or just a movement. Paula watched her, perhaps expecting more of a response. When it didn't come, she went into her bedroom.

Shelby poured herself a cup of coffee from the porcelain coffee service.

"You don't have to stay with me," I said. "Anyway, I want to track down a friend of mine who's visiting here, too."

I didn't really expect an answer. Shelby wasn't exactly a gold-medal conversationalist. So I choked on my tea when she said, "Where's she staying?"

I coughed and didn't bother to tell her my friend was Spike. "In an area called Bloomsbury. I can look it up on the map."

"I know where it is," Shelby said. "It's near the British Museum. We could go see the mummies. They're cool."

Somehow I wasn't surprised that Shelby would like mummies.

"We can take the Tube from Marble Arch," Shelby said with more interest than she'd shown in anything except high tea, "and get out at Holborn. Or change there and get out at Russell Square. It's easy."

"I got the impression you'd just as soon be alone today."

"I just don't want to go anywhere with her"—she nodded toward the bedroom door. "Or him." There was no need to clarify who *him* was.

"Me, neither," I said.

Shelby looked at me for a moment, then drained her coffee cup and said, "Let's go."

"Have you got any money?" I asked. "Because I do if you don't."

"She gave me some. I won't take any from him. It makes him crazy that he can't buy me."

Buy her? Is that what he was trying to do with me?

Shelby grabbed a crumpled black denim jacket from the back of her chair and we left without saying goodbye to Paula.

It seemed that Shelby really did remember everything from her previous trip to London, or else she'd been secretly boning up, because she knew exactly how to use the Underground. She steered me through a turnstile, down long tiled tunnels and onto a platform where a train was just arriving. We boarded and I sat knee-to-knee with a person of indeterminate sex, dressed all in leopard skin from boots to eyeglass frames, reading aloud from a book held upside down.

I was glad to surface at our stop: all those tons of earth over my head, trapping me underground with strange, foreign creatures, had caused a panicky feeling in my stomach. Oddly, at the same time, I'd felt rather worldly and daring.

We found Spike's hotel, a huge, ugly building with no style whatsoever and a lobby full of milling tour groups of every nationality. The harried clerk at the check-in desk told me that Spike's group was out—in the European style, they'd all deposited their room keys at the desk when they left the hotel.

I was so frustrated I wanted to kick the desk. I was standing in his hotel mere feet from where he might have been and he wasn't there. Even though it had been less than three days since I'd seen him, it had been on another continent, in another time zone, and might as well have been three glacial epochs ago.

"She must be your best friend," Shelby said, paying more attention to me than I realized.

"It's not a she," I said. "It's my . . ." I didn't know what to call Spike. *Boyfriend* sounded frivolous and juvenile. *Significant other* was too impersonal. *Friend* wasn't personal enough.

"Your main man?" Shelby supplied.

"I guess."

"Why don't you leave him a message? Have him   89

call you at our hotel. Ask him to have dinner with us. I'd just as soon not dine only with her and him."

"You think that would be okay?"

Incredulous, she looked at me. "Who cares? Just do it."

So I did.

Then we went to the British Museum, which was full of things—like the Rosetta Stone and the Magna Carta and the Gutenberg Bible—that I'd heard about but somehow didn't actually believe existed. I loved the illuminated medieval manuscripts, their pages full of indecipherable writing and tiny pictures of birds and flowers and Bible scenes done in gilt and glowing colors. Such painstaking, blinding, exalting effort, still potent in a time the artists couldn't even have dreamed of.

Shelby was fascinated by the ancient jewelry. We stood before cases of exquisite Sumerian pieces and pectorals from Egyptian tombs and Scythian gold, while she said, nearly reverently, "Wow. Somebody really wore those. Somebody my age. Somebody who's just dust now." I wondered if someday Mitzi's favorite plastic palm-tree earrings would be in a display case in some twenty-fifth-century museum.

We bought sandwiches and tea in the stuffy lunchroom of the museum and sat at a little table under a sign warning us of pickpockets.

"I'm glad we came here," I said. "I don't usually think of museums as being so interesting."

"My father's hobby was classical history," Shelby said. "He loved museums. *She* isn't interested in anything antique unless it's part of interior decorating, so he used to take me with him and tell me stories about what we saw. Almost everything was once really important to somebody in an everyday sort of way. It knocks me out to think of that. And I wouldn't know any of that if my father hadn't told me."

"You were lucky," I said, biting into a ham-and-butter sandwich on big square bread.

"For a while," Shelby said.

After lunch we wandered around Bloomsbury, looking in shop windows, feeling the feeble English sun on our shoulders.

In front of a shop with a black-and-silver sign reading SIXTH DIMENSION over the door, Shelby grabbed my arm and dragged me inside. The shop was about the size of my bedroom at home. A wizened woman in a sari sat on a stool in a dark corner, surveying the small space stuffed with Indian jewelry, clothing, scarves, incense, bells, tiny carved pipes.

"These must be useless," I said, pointing to the pipes. "They look like they'd only be good for about one puff."

"They are," Shelby answered. "They're hashish pipes."

"Hashish!" I whispered, wondering how Shelby knew. "Is that legal here?"

"No," Shelby said. "But this is a big city, an inter-

91

national city, like Los Angeles or New York. You can probably find anything you want here, just like you can there."

"Are you ready to go?" I asked, hopelessly rabbit-hearted.

"No," Shelby said, unconcerned that we were in a place of silken, unwholesome allure. "I want to buy something. Look at these earrings. They look sort of like those Etruscan ones at the museum, don't they? I think I'll get them. Relax," she added, studying me. "This is a cool place."

While Shelby bought the earrings, chatting with the Indian woman more pleasantly than I'd heard her talk to either Paula or my father, I found a gauzy scarf shot with silver threads I thought Lily would like. And some incense for Nell, and a complicated pair of earrings for Mitzi. I might have been able to find the same things at an import store in San Diego, but these, I could brag, came directly from England, the mother of colonies, from a dark and mysterious shop which might not even be here tomorrow.

And I needed to do something to make me feel linked to people I loved, to home.

"You should get some of those earrings for yourself," Shelby said as I paid for my purchases.

"They're not my style. I like little ones. These are too dangly."

"You could stand to loosen up. Not look so much like a PTA president."

I stiffened as Shelby yawned, apparently not aware, or not caring, that she'd hurt my feelings. "I need a nap," she said. "I don't care what he says about jet lag. By body time it's 8 A.M. and my body knows it."

We didn't talk on the way back to the hotel. I didn't want to give her another opportunity to say something I wouldn't like hearing. Until she'd made that remark in the Sixth Dimension, I'd started to think we might be able to get along. Silly me.

There was a message from Spike waiting for me at the hotel, saying he'd meet me there at six-thirty, which seemed like a year away.

I lay on my bed wondering if there were girls on his tour who didn't look like PTA presidents, girls who would suit him better than I did, until I fell asleep.

When I woke, I was alone in the bedroom and I could hear Shelby and Paula in the sitting room.

"I don't care how fabulous a sleigh bed it is," Shelby said, drawing out the word *fabulous* until it sounded like nonsense. "I told you I didn't want any new furniture. Put it in one of the other rooms."

"I don't see why you want to hang on to your old things," Paula said. "You've had them for years. They're for a little child."

"Daddy let me pick them out myself. I liked them then and I still like them. They're mine. Who knows how many other people have slept, or God knows what else, in that sleigh bed?"

"But that's the charm of antiques," Paula said, 93

forced patience in her voice. "They've been touched by other people's lives. They have resonance."

"Not to me."

Was this the same girl who found it fascinating to think of who had worn the Roman bracelets in the British Museum?

"Anyway," Shelby added, "if I hang on to my stuff long enough, they'll be antiques and you'll be *begging* me to keep them."

"You are impossible," Paula said in a soft voice with a hard edge to it.

"Thanks," Shelby said, and pushed open the door into our bedroom. I pretended to be asleep.

She joggled my bed with her silver-pointed boot, and when I opened my eyes, she said, "It's almost six. Your squeeze'll be here soon."

Thank God.

I got up and went through the sitting room to knock on the door of my father's bedroom. Then, without opening the door, I called, "I invited my friend to have dinner with us tonight." I refused to ask him if that was all right. It was more than all right with me.

"Good," he called. "That's fine. I'm glad you found her. Our reservation's at seven-thirty."

"He'll be here at six-thirty," I said and walked back to my room to dress.

I heard my father's faint voice saying, "He?"

10

*W*hen Spike arrived, exactly at six-thirty, he looked so good to me, so American, so particularly Californian, I thought *he* should be on display in some museum.

My father shook his hand and Paula began wrapping him up in her cool stream of social conversation and Shelby watched him in a measuring, almost predatory way.

For the occasion of dinner out, with Paula in a silk dress and me in a knit top and skirt, Shelby had changed into white jeans, a man's white T-shirt, a black leather jacket heavy with stainless steel, her boots, and her new Indian earrings. There was a possibility she had also combed her hair.

Our dinner conversation, minus any contribution from Shelby, was the nondescript sort made by strangers who never expect to see each other again.

"We went to the National Gallery today," Spike told us. "You should try to go. The Rembrandts are too much. They even have X rays of them showing how he painted the bone structure before he painted the faces."

"So you're an art lover?" Paula asked.

"Not until now," he said, drinking a whole glass of water. We were eating Indian food, and while we were used to the spiciness of Mexican food at home, this was a new and painful spiciness. "I liked how thorough he was. How careful he was about what he was doing."

So sometimes it was all right to be very careful. It wasn't always something only PTA presidents did.

It seemed as if this dinner of fiery flavors and bland conversation would never end. All I wanted was to be alone with Spike, to recapture how things had been three days ago, before I left my real life behind.

When at last we left the restaurant, it was into a misty drizzle so fine it didn't seem to be falling but merely hanging in the air. Shelby, who had remained silent, though watchful and assessing of Spike, put two fingers in her mouth and whistled so loud that a cab stopped immediately in front of us.

96

"Awesome," Spike said, giving her a look of admiration that she returned with a shrug and an appraising gaze. I wanted to grab Spike and run.

"Can we drop you at your hotel?" my father asked Spike as we stood by the open cab door, Paula holding her purse over her head to protect her hair.

"No!" I said, and they all looked at me. "We're going to take a walk," I said more moderately. This was news to Spike. But I wasn't ready to say good night to him yet. Especially not in front of my—whatever they were. I certainly wasn't going to call them my family.

"In the rain?" Paula asked, raising her fine eyebrows.

"We can pick up an umbrella at our hotel. It always rains in England. It's not a big deal, the way it is in Southern California." I just wanted everybody to shut up and go away so I could be alone with Spike.

Shelby volunteered to wait in the lobby with Spike while I went up to get the umbrella. What could I say? Don't touch him, don't even look at him, he's mine? I couldn't say why her interest in Spike made me so nervous. She wasn't likely to dazzle him with her conversational skills. But I'd abandoned my familiar routines to come on this trip—my friends and my cats and my job—and then found that my father had been appropriated by people he preferred to me—and was annoyed with myself for caring—and I wasn't about to have one more thing that was mine threatened.

"Bye, Shelby," I said, when I returned with the   97

umbrella, taking Spike's arm and pulling him toward the door.

"Yeah, bye," Spike said hastily over his shoulder. "Enjoy your trip."

Once outside, I wrapped my arms around Spike's waist before I opened the umbrella, pressing my cheek against his sweater and breathing in his scent. "Oh, I've been wanting to do this all night," I said. "I've missed you so much."

His arms tightened around me. "Me, too. I thought dinner would never be over. And that food *hurt*."

Pretty soon, we realized we were getting wet, so we opened the umbrella and walked slowly along the rainy streets, our arms around each other.

"Your dad looks like a movie star," Spike said. "No wonder you're so beautiful. But where did the wife and Shelby the Silent come from? I didn't know they were going with you."

"Neither did I. A little surprise he sprang on me at the airport."

"At the airport? Pretty tricky. Why didn't he tell you, did he say?"

"He says he was afraid I wouldn't have come if I'd known about them. And he's right. He wants us all to be one big happy family."

"You don't have to." He kissed my temple. "You have a family already."

"I know," I said. Tears pricked behind my eyes.

"It's so strange and awful. I always wanted him to

think I was wonderful, his own darling daughter, the apple of both of his eyes, and now he's only taking an interest in me because he's suddenly decided he wants to be a family man. I'm mad at him because he wasn't interested enough in me before and because he's too interested in me now. But not in the way I want him to be interested in me. And for the wrong reasons." I laughed shortly. "Nothing he does pleases me and still I want him to do more of it."

"I get it," Spike said. "Would he, if you told him?"

"Unlikely. And then I worry about stupid things like you getting charmed by some girl on your trip, or by Shelby because she can whistle better than I can."

Spike steered me into a doorway and propped the umbrella in the corner. He held me and stroked my wet hair. "Good whistling abilities usually are something I look for in a girlfriend," he said, "but somehow you've captured me without that." He held me away from him and looked into my face. "Berkeley, get serious. *Shelby?*"

I pressed my embarrassed face against his shoulder. "What about the girls on your trip?"

"I haven't checked out their whistling yet," he said into my ear. "I'll have to let you know if it's over between us once I have."

That started the tears. I felt like such an idiot, but I couldn't help it. "I want to go home," I cried. "I want to go with you. My own father doesn't even like me. Neither does Shelby." I was talking through 99 sobby hiccups now, feeling more like a fool than ever. "They think I'm boring. I have to know when I'll see you again."

He held me and murmured words I couldn't hear because of my own crying, and kissed my forehead and my cheeks and my hair. Gradually I calmed down.

"I'm sorry," I said, afraid I would start crying again. "I didn't mean to do that. It's just, I was so . . . I haven't been able to talk to anybody for . . ."

"It's okay," he said. "It is." He ran his hand up and down my back.

"Oh, I don't deserve you."

"Yes, you do. I'm a superior person and everyone deserves somebody like that." When I raised my head to look at him, he said, "Just kidding. A little joke to make you laugh. But, Berkeley, *you're* a superior person. You'll get through this. Remember, you don't *have* to like him just because he's your father. Or you can like some things about him without liking everything, the way I can admire Shelby's whistling without being the slightest bit interested in her."

I nodded, bumping my head against his chest. I was hardly listening. All I wanted was for him to keep holding me, keep talking to me. Lily was right; this was much better than just having a good time with a great-looking guy.

"After all, loving has as much to do with the lovee as with the lover," he went on. "There's a certain way each of us wants to be loved. And not all the people who love us will do it that way. But love is still love, even if it isn't the kind you had in mind. You can appreciate it and still keep looking for what you need somewhere else."

"You're what I need," I said, pulling his head down so I could kiss him.

When we finally stepped out of the doorway onto the sidewalk again, the rain had almost stopped. I walked Spike to the Tube stop to go back to his hotel and didn't want to let him disappear down the stairs. "When?" I asked.

"I don't know. We have day trips out to Stonehenge and Stratford-upon-Avon and some other places. I'll have to call you." He kissed me. "It'll be okay. *I* love you, even if nobody else does. Ah, that's my girl. When you smile like that, I want to—" Playfully, he nipped at my neck.

I felt an actual, physical pain in my chest when he went down the stairs and into the Tube station. All the way back to the hotel, I dragged the point of the umbrella behind me, wincing at the tooth-jarring noise it made.

Before I went to sleep, I wrote to Lily.

Dear Lily,

Today I went to the British Museum and got you something pretty in a funky shop. Spike had dinner with us, thank goodness.

101

Love to you and Madge and Wuffums and Nell and Grady and Mitzi.

Berkeley

11

The next morning my father woke Shelby and me. He was dressed and polished, glowing with energy.

"Up, girls, up! No meetings for me today. We can do museums, Crown Jewels, guards changing, a great high tea someplace. I've had my run in Hyde Park and it's a beautiful day." He jerked open the window drapes and sunshine flooded in. "I'll bring you each a nice cuppa to get you started."

"What time is it?" I mumbled.

"And what the hell is a cuppa?" Shelby asked, pulling her head out from under her pillow.

"It's nine and a cuppa is a cup of tea," he said before he left the room.

"That means it's 1 A.M. body time," I said, rolling on my back and squinting at the sun. My eyes were still swollen from crying so much last night.

"God," Shelby said, rubbing her face. "He's like that every morning. It makes me want to poison him."

It was strange to think that Shelby knew more about my father than I did. "Your father wasn't that way?" I asked.

Shelby sat up and leaned against the headboard. She shook her head. "He's like me. We prefer to sneak up on the day. No head-on collisions. We're at our best at night."

Shelby's best didn't seem much different from her worst, in my opinion. I wondered if she realized she was using the present tense about her father. "And Paula?" I asked, working on the knot of my father's life without me.

"She says it's undignified to have ups and downs. If you ask me, she's afraid to." She yawned so hugely I was afraid she was going to unhinge her jaw.

"Afraid? Why?" Having just experienced a major down of my own, I didn't see how you could avoid having them, even if you wanted to. They had an irresistible force of their own.

"She likes being taken care of. She doesn't want to endanger that."

I remembered Paula's father had died when she was a little girl. Hadn't there been anybody to take care of her then, the way I'd had Lily? With last night's experience with Spike still vivid in my mind, I said, "People who love you keep doing it even when you're having ups and downs."

"Try and tell her that. She's not great at it herself."

"Well, they can get exasperated," I added, thinking how hard it must be to be Shelby's mother, "but love is pretty sturdy." It had been with Lily and me, anyway. Which made me wonder what to call what my father felt—or didn't feel—for me.

My father bustled back into the bedroom with a tea tray. "Much as I like to see my ladies sharing girl talk," he said, "breakfast's on the way and I need to see your shining faces in the sitting room pronto." He left.

"I think I'm going to puke," Shelby said.

I agreed. But thirty minutes later we were both showered—I was relieved that Shelby at last took one —dressed, and at the breakfast table, though we weren't shining.

"We'll start with the Tower," my father said as he dug into his kippers and eggs. "I know Paula wants to see the Crown Jewels. Probably like to have a few of them." He winked at her and she gave him a soft smile. "I'd like to see Henry VIII's armor, too. It's supposed to weigh over one hundred pounds. I pity the poor horse that had to carry him *and* the armor. I've got a few other things in mind to fill the day." He took a healthy mouthful of eggs.

"I've been to the Tower," Shelby said.

"You were a little girl then," Paula told her.

"My favorite thing was Henry VIII's armored cod-piece," Shelby remarked. "Big as a mixing bowl."

"Shelby, really," Paula said, frowning at her.

My father cleared his throat and put his napkin on the table. "Well, all right, then, let's get going."

"I'm not finished," Shelby said, taking a minute bite of toast.

Paula rolled her eyes and excused herself. She went into her bedroom and closed the door.

It took Shelby almost ten minutes to finish her slice of toast. When she finally did, my father said, "We'll take the Tube. It's part of the adventure of London. You can't go everywhere in a cab."

"Goody," Shelby said under her breath. "An adventure."

As we made our way through the tiled tunnels of the Underground, Shelby said to my father, "This is the wrong side. It takes us away from the Tower, not toward it."

I had no idea. I can figure out a map if I have unlimited time and no distractions, but in a situation like this I was as map-impaired as I'd ever been, and I had simply been following blindly along.

My father stopped and studied the map while Shelby looked off into the black tunnel and tapped the toe of her boot. Paula stood calmly by, waiting for the 106 conflict to be resolved without her participation.

"You know," he finally said, over the sound of a train thundering into the station, "I think you're right. It's the next platform over for the train to the Tower."

Shelby turned on her heel and stalked across to the proper platform with Paula following her. When I made a motion to go after her, my father took my arm and pulled me through the open door of the train stopped in front of us. Even as we boarded, he called to Paula, "I'll meet you at the hotel after lunch."

The last thing I saw through the train window as we roared away was Paula's surprised face in the distance, her perfectly lipsticked mouth in an O, her perfectly plucked eyebrows arched toward her hairline. I wondered if she would be able to keep her ups and downs under control now.

"What are you doing?" I asked my father in amazement.

"You and I are going to take a ride," he said.

"But why? Where are we going?"

"Look at the map." He pointed to the map of stations posted above the windows. "Anywhere. It doesn't matter. How about Holland Park?"

Even though I felt as if I were being kidnapped, in a curious way I was thrilled that he had singled me out. It was *me* he had kidnapped, not Paula or Shelby.

"But what about Paula and Shelby?" I asked, raising my voice to be heard above the roar and clatter of the train.

"They'll find something to do, don't worry about them." He looked around, apparently unconcerned.

"I don't get this," I said.

"Wait," he said. "We can't talk here. It's too noisy. Wait'll we get to the park."

Waiting was all I could do, marking off the stations until we got to Holland Park, wondering if I could find my way back to the hotel by myself if I had to, if this excursion turned out to be something I wasn't going to like.

We emerged from the Underground, crossed Holland Park Avenue, and entered the park. It was cool and green there; flower beds blooming away, geese in a pond fighting over bread tossed to them by children with round pink cheeks.

"Sit down," my father said, directing me to a bench and seating himself.

I stayed on my feet.

"Come on," he said. "I want to talk to you."

"What about?"

"We've gotten off to a bad start on this trip. I don't want it to get worse."

I sat on the edge of the bench, a yard away from him. "Then why didn't you just tell Paula you wanted to talk to me? Why did you do it the way you did it?"

"I didn't have a plan until the second before I got on that train. Don't worry. Paula will understand. She knows I can be impulsive. Life's more interesting that way."

For him, maybe.

Paula might put up with it for whatever sick or sad reasons she had, but I definitely did not have to. I'd seen all I wanted to of his practice of fatherhood by impulse.

"I know I was wrong not to tell you about Paula and Shelby coming. But I thought once you met them, once you and Shelby were sisters—"

"Oh, stop," I said, cutting him off. "Shelby and I aren't sisters. We don't even like each other. And from what I can tell, she doesn't like you or Paula either. What could possibly have made you think this would work?"

"It *could* work. If we all tried." He gave me that Hollywood smile. "Why not chance it?"

"Why should I?" I seemed to have uncorked a batch of feelings I'd had bottled up too long and they were dying to get out. Maybe it was the emotional upheaval I'd had the night before with Spike that had released them. Maybe it was Shelby's example of free-floating obnoxiousness. No lightning bolt had hit either one of us for our flagrant behavior. Might as well enjoy the full range of feelings before one did. There was a sense of danger and of thrill to this emotional muscle-flexing. If that's what Lily meant by my learning to stretch myself, maybe she was right. If it's what Mitzi meant by feeling fizzy, wide-eyed, and all there, she was right, too.

"So I can be more of a father to you," he said with

a straight face. "So we can be more of a family." I had to restrain myself from jeering.

In an equally sincere voice, I said, "And what was preventing you from being more of a father to me before Paula came along?"

"Oh, Berkeley, give me a chance. I was young, I was heedless, I was self-centered, I was a lot of things. I've changed."

"Too bad you couldn't have come to this realization about fifteen years ago. Then it might have done me some good."

He ran his hand through his hair. "I never guessed you were so angry with me. It never showed when I saw you."

"Maybe you should have seen me more often. I was so afraid of scaring you away permanently I was on my best behavior, not that it did any good." I watched a park cat crouched in the bushes eyeing three little birds hopping and pecking on the path in front of her. I didn't feel a bit of sympathy for those birds: any-thing so clueless, so stupid, so *heedless* deserved to be pounced on. I admired the cat for being so crafty, so single-minded, so strong.

"Okay." He stuck his hands in his jacket pockets. "Paula said this might happen. I deserve it, I guess. But what's to keep us from starting fresh now? You're still my child."

"Your child?" I stood up to give myself more room to breathe, I felt so full of . . . of . . . I don't know what, but it was almost suffocating me. "Don't you know it takes more than some chromosomes to make you my father?" The cat, inching toward the birds, caught my eye. Had it inherited some ancestor's slyness, speed, strength? What part of me had come from my father? Did the fact that I'd initially allowed him to think Spike was a female friend mean I'd inherited his indirect, scheming qualities? Did the way I was acting now show I'd inherited some of his risk-taking flamboyance?

"I know I can't go back and buy you your first bike or ice-cream cone or party dress. I wish I could. Okay, I blew that part. I have to try to be your father now. Whether it works is up to you."

I was having an even harder time catching my breath. "Oh, no, you don't. You don't create the problem and then make it my job to fix it."

He stood now, too, and took a step toward me. I backed up. "What can I do?" He really looked pained. The same way he'd looked in the airport when he'd begged me to come on this trip. Because he needed me. Ha. "Do you want me to pay for all your college expenses? I will. No problem."

"Does everything come down to whether you can buy it or not? Bikes and dresses and college and trips? What about the other stuff?"

"Other stuff?"

"You don't even know if I'm *going* to college. You never asked. You don't know anything about me." 111

Two apple-cheeked children near us stopped throwing their ball and stood staring at me. "You've never asked me a single question about myself. *That's* the other stuff."

"*Are* you going to college?" he asked.

The children's mother took their hands and led them away, looking back at us over her shoulder. The cat watched big-eyed from the bushes. The birds pecked, oblivious.

"What do you think?" Now I was breathing hard, as if I'd been running.

"I think you are," he said. "You're bright. You have an ambitious mother, a good role model even if I haven't been. You're college material. If you're not going, you should be."

I wanted him to give up, to put me on a plane for home, to admit that we couldn't get along and never would be able to. When he kept trying, in his blind, clumsy way, to make a truce with me, my lioness hesitated in her pursuit.

He sensed it the minute I did. No wonder he'd been such a success at selling insurance. He knew just when to move in and close the sale.

"I know you're going to college," he said, his shoulders relaxing. "And it will be my privilege to send you there, no matter where it is, Harvard or Stanford or anywhere."

I shook my head in admiration. It was what I had told Spike—I didn't like what my father was doing, and I wanted him to keep doing it. I wanted him to want me, to finally be interested in me. And then I wanted to spurn him, to do to him what he had done to me for seventeen years.

I wanted him to continue, to ask me why I'd picked UCLA, what I wanted to major in, even why I wanted to go to college in the first place.

"Pubs should be open now," he said, coming toward me and taking my arm in his possessive way. The startled birds flew off and the cat, peering from the bushes, glared at my father for allowing them unmindful escape. "I'll buy you a ploughman's lunch that I guarantee will sit like a stone in your stomach all day."

I couldn't figure out why that should be a recommendation for a meal, but, like a convict who'd almost made a getaway, I let him lead me from the park. If nothing else, contact with my father seemed to have taught me how to talk to someone face-to-face about something difficult. He needed watching.

12

*B*ack at the hotel after lunch that, oddly, had been fun, thanks to my father's high spirits and his willingness to joke with everybody in the pub—as well as buy a pint of ale all around—we found that neither Paula nor Shelby had returned yet.

I called Spike, who was off with his group until well after dinner, according to the hotel desk clerk, and took a nap, my stomach as heavy as my father had promised.

When Paula came in about teatime, loaded with packages, Shelby wasn't with her. "She jumped on the next train that came through the station," Paula said, "and went God knows where, while I stood there watching."

"Do you want me to call the police?" my father asked. "She's never done this in a strange city before."

"No, of course not," Paula said. "She's perfectly capable of finding her way home. She's just trying to drive me crazy." She turned to the telephone. "I'd better see if my dress has been pressed for tonight." She and Ace were going to some kind of business dinner.

She never once mentioned my father's desertion of her in the Tube station.

At six-thirty, while Paula soaked in the bath, Shelby came sauntering in.

"Where have you been?" my father asked. "Your mother's been worried."

Shelby gave him a skeptical look. "Seeing the sights. I don't wear a watch, so I didn't know what time it was."

"You have to be careful here," he said. "London's a big city. Anything could happen."

"So's L.A. Where I live." She went into our bedroom.

At eight, when Ace and Paula left for their dinner, splendid in tuxedo, silk, and jewels, Shelby was still shut up in there.

"I don't know when we'll be back," he said to me,

as I sat reading guidebooks and picking through a sumptuous room-service dinner he'd ordered for Shelby and me.

I nodded and automatically said, "Have a good time."

As soon as the door closed behind them, Shelby came out of the bedroom. "I thought they'd never leave," she said.

"Want some dinner?" I indicated the banquet spread out on the table.

She picked up a roll and, still standing, spread it with butter and laid a slice of chicken on it. "I'm going out," she said with a full mouth.

"Where?"

"Dancing. Want to come? Want to call your hunk-o-matic boyfriend?"

"Dancing?" I repeated stupidly. She didn't know a soul in London. How could she be going dancing?

"I met some guys this afternoon in a pub. They told me about this place in Camden Town. It's supposed to be *the* place."

"Spike can't go. He's off with his tour someplace."

"So go without him."

After a long pause, while I weighed all the reasons I shouldn't, my lioness said, "Why not?" Was I supposed to sit around reading guidebooks like a . . . like a PTA president while everybody else got to kick up their heels?

"All *right*," Shelby said. "But you can't go like that."

"Like what?"

"Looking the way you do, all buttoned up. I'll have to mess you up a little. Come into the bedroom."

"Mess me up?" But I followed her anyway.

"First, clothes," Shelby was saying, flipping through the few things in my side of the closet. "Black is best. Don't you have anything black? Ah, here, a black skirt. But it's too long. Roll it up at the waist and we can belt it."

By the time she was finished, I was outfitted in black tights, a very short black skirt with a white T-shirt belted over it, and Shelby's black denim jacket. She had gelled my hair and pulled it out into points around my face, loaned me her Indian earrings, and outlined my eyes and mouth with heavy color. When I looked into the mirror, I didn't know who it was I saw.

Shelby wore all black, topped with her leather jacket, and when we left the hotel the doorman gave us a look that seemed compounded of equal parts amusement and fear.

We rode the Tube, silent, sullen, with a whiff of the outlaw about us. I was wearing not only a new costume but a new possibility, a test flight into Shelby's life.

It was raining again when we came out of the Tube station, a fine misty rain that fuzzed the streetlights.

"Pull your jacket up over your head," Shelby commanded, "or your hair'll collapse."

We knew we'd reached our destination by the number of people, most in various combinations of leather and black clothing, who stood on the sidewalk and spilled into the street, smoking and talking to each other in accents incomprehensible to me. After we paid our admission, Shelby, with me right behind her, elbowed her way into a big, dark, low-ceilinged room hazy and reeking with cigarette smoke. It was packed with people sitting at tables around a jammed and writhing dance floor, ringing with the din of music and shouted conversation.

Just as I caught up with Shelby, a tall thin creature with dead-white skin and long black hair loomed before me. "Dance, luv?" he said and took my hand, pulling me to the edge of the dance floor. I congratulated Shelby for putting together a disguise for me that must be perfect.

"I'll get us a drink," Shelby shouted over the music. "Come back here when you're done."

Actual dancing, as I knew it, was impossible in the thick crowd, so we bobbed about, knocking into people with every movement. My funereal partner kept yelling things to me, things that might have been questions, but between the noise and his accent, I couldn't understand anything he said. I nodded and bobbed and looked at the people dancing around me in outfits ranging from the merely menacing to the almost obscene and reminded myself that I looked nearly as scary as they did. There was a peculiar sort of camaraderie in the realization.

When the music stopped, I gave my partner a little

wave, probably enough out of keeping with my image as to blow my cover, and wedged away from him through the crowd. There was no future in hanging out with a guy whose speech was unintelligible.

Shelby was standing where I'd left her, holding two pints of beer. She handed them both to me while she lit a cigarette, and then took one back.

"I didn't know you smoked," I said, taking a sip of the strong, sour beer. I wished I'd asked for a lemon squash, like the one I'd had at the pub.

"When the occasion calls for it," she said.

Someone in a leather suit cruised by and asked me to dance. I shook my head and raised my glass to him and he navigated away. I wondered what Spike would think if he could see me. I knew Mitzi would love this place.

A man with a Caribbean lilt in his voice came up to us and said, "Want anything, ladies?"

"Not now," Shelby said. "Thanks." And he drifted off into the crowd.

"What did he mean?" I asked.

"Drugs."

"They sell drugs here?" My voice went up with the music. "How do you know?"

"I just know. Everybody here is probably high on something. That guy screaming over there in the corner? That's not just because he's having such a good time."

A boy with long blond hair sat in a chair at a corner   119 table, his head back, screaming up at the ceiling, while his tablemates ignored him. The noise in the room was so dense I couldn't hear him, but the distended veins in his neck showed how hard he was yelling. Near him, a guy dressed only in high-heeled black boots and a leather jockstrap studded with rhinestones stood holding a blue-dyed poodle and talking to a girl with a pink Mohawk haircut and black lipstick.

When I turned back from these inspiring sights, Shelby was gone. Peering through the smoke, I finally spotted her on the dance floor. She was still holding her beer glass and her cigarette.

She danced for a long time. I put my glass of warm flat beer on the floor and refused everybody who asked me to dance. I wanted to go back to the hotel. It wasn't that I was afraid or intimidated. I'd gaped all I could at the amazements this place had to offer, and now I was bored.

When Shelby returned, she was sweaty and exhilarated. "Want another beer?" she asked. "I'm dying of thirst."

"No, thanks. I'm going to head back to the hotel."

"We just got here. You chickening out already?"

"I'm not chickening out. The smoke hurts my eyes and the music is deafening."

"Quit being such an old maid. Get into it."

My lioness was quiet. My rabbit was quiet. It was me who spoke. "This isn't what I prefer to get into. I'm going."

"Fine," Shelby answered. "I'll see you later."

"You're staying?"

"I'm having fun. Feel free to fink out if you want."

I thought of mentioning to her that I didn't think it was such a good idea for her to stay here by herself, but I knew what she'd say to that. I thought of explaining to her that finking out was different from making a choice based on personal preference, but I knew how she'd take that, too.

It wasn't my job to keep this kamikaze kid from self-destructing. I was leaving. As I turned away from her, Shelby said, "You're really going?"

I turned back. "You didn't believe me?"

"No, I—okay, whatever. I'll see you later."

Rain still fizzled and misted outside, but I didn't bother to pull my jacket over my head. I didn't care if my hair drooped. I'd laboriously puzzled out the route map and was already on the train when Shelby came running through the archway, across the platform, and between the doors just before they closed. We rode home in complete silence.

We came quietly into the suite, not sure whether my father and Paula were home yet. An umbrella, opened to dry in front of the fireplace, indicated they were, and we could hear the murmur of the TV from their bedroom.

I couldn't figure out why they weren't up worrying where we were, until I spotted a note, taped to our bedroom door, reading "Please come in quietly. We've gone to bed."

I washed my face and brushed the gel out of my hair. Why had Shelby come back to the hotel with me? Could it be that she was just a lonely kid who occasionally scared herself with her own rebellion? Or did her mind work so differently from mine that I would never figure her out?

Before I went to bed, I wrote to Lily.

Dear Lily,

I went to a London dance club tonight. There was enough leather there to give a vegetarian nightmares. And enough other bizarre stuff to give them to everybody else.

Love, Berkeley

13

The next day Paula did her duty by Shelby and me while my father was off doing something to further international harmony in the insurance game. We blitzed through Westminster Abbey, the guard-changing at Buckingham Palace, and the National Portrait Gallery (just the mezzanine for the portraits of the royal family), catching a glimpse of Big Ben and Trafalgar Square on the way. The only time she slowed down was to look in shop windows.

Shelby was mum as a clam, so Paula lavished her flood of small talk on me. It had a hypnotic, soothing effect and I could feel myself being drawn to her by the spider strands of her focused attention.

We met Ace for tea at the Ritz. Apparently, his day had gone well, because he was jovial and expansive and he carried a big green-and-gold bag from Harrods department store.

"Hello, ladies," he greeted us. "Don't you look gorgeous with your pretty heads stuffed full of sights."

Shelby snorted.

"What's in the bag, Ace?" Paula asked.

"Gifts for my ladies." He ordered our tea and then reached into the bag. "Paula, my dear, for you." He handed her a long, flat box.

She turned it over and over, as if she could divine what was in it, as my father distributed identical big rectangular boxes to Shelby and me. Shelby deposited hers under her chair and dug into the tea cakes which had just arrived. My father's attention went from her to Paula, who was carefully undoing her package, folding and smoothing the paper as if she were going to save it, winding the gold twine into a loop around her fingers. In her box was a velvet case and in that was a bracelet of gold links and glittering stones. Paula sucked in her breath and then breathed out, "Oh, Ace. It's fabulous." She held her wrist and the bracelet out to him and he fastened it for her.

"Do you like it?" he asked.

124   "What a question," she said, looking at him with an

adoring and slightly dazed expression. I'd probably look dazed, too, if somebody had handed me a bauble like that, but I'd have thought Paula would be used to it by now. I wondered if her first husband had been able to do such things for her.

"Go on, Berkeley," Paula said. "Open yours."

I did. It was a cashmere sweater in a heavenly shade of periwinkle blue, another high-stakes bribe. "It's beautiful," I said. "Thank you." I knew he wanted more from me, but what he wanted couldn't be bought, not with sweaters or trips or anything with a dollar sign on it.

Shelby kept her attention on her meal.

"Aren't you going to open your present, Shelby?" her mother asked.

"I already know what it is and I don't want it," she said.

"You know what it is?" my father asked.

"Yeah. It's a cashmere sweater. Like Berkeley's, except it's probably a different color." She put a whole tea-sized cucumber sandwich in her mouth.

"How do you know that?" he asked, but from the strained smile on his face, I knew she was right.

"Because you lump us together as 'daughters' or 'sisters' or whatever, and so you get us the same things."

"What's wrong with that?" he asked. "You both *are* daughters."

"But we're not the same." She shook her head as if   125

there was no use expecting him to understand this. She was probably right. "In case you haven't noticed, a cashmere sweater is not exactly my style."

"But you'd look good in one," he said. "Why not try something different? You might like it."

I could see her stiffen, the same way I did when he tried to persuade me that he knew what was good for me. Then she made a sound, maybe a private laugh, and went on with her tea.

Paula came to the rescue with exclamations about her bracelet and then a travelogue about what we'd done that day.

When we got ready to leave, Shelby went off without retrieving her package from under her chair. Paula picked it up and brought it along.

Back at the hotel, there was a message for me to call Spike, but by the time I did, he was gone again. Apparently, while I was doing this, Paula had slipped into our room and left the box on Shelby's bed. When Shelby found it, she sailed it across the room, where it hit the closet door and fell, dented, to the floor.

I sat on my bed, my back against the headboard, my knees drawn up. "What's your biggest complaint about him?" I asked.

She turned, her eyes glittering. With tears? With rage? I couldn't tell. "That he's not my father. That he's such an arrogant, self-assured overachiever. That he won't make it easy by hating me back. That Paula married him so soon after my father died. Is that enough, or do you want more?"

"There's more?"

"That he's so much more successful than my father was and can afford to do these things that Daddy would have loved to do. That he keeps trying to make friends with me. You."

"Me? What did I do?"

"You have his same look, that beautiful, rich, satisfied look."

I sat up with a jerk. "Shelby. I'm not any of those things. He may be, but I'm not."

"Oh, sure," she said. "You've got your shiny hair and your perfect skin and your hunk-o-rama boyfriend and whoever all those people are you write postcards to."

"I went to a dermatologist for two years before my skin cleared up, and I'm not crazy about Spike because of how he looks, and I'm mostly writing to my mother, who I've had plenty of fights with. And I worry about a lot of things."

She was looking out the window with her back to me. "He's still alive."

"My father? That's true, but he might as well be dead for all the good he's done me."

She turned to face me, her face anguished. "But he's still *alive*. Don't you get it? Even if you don't see him, you know he's out there in the world somewhere, living."

127

I said carefully, "You must have loved your dad a lot."

She looked out the window again, making a sound that was almost a moan. "He thought I was terrific."

I understood the value of that. I had learned it from Lily, who had armored me with her love. I was sure of it in the fibers of my muscles, in the beat of my heart; I knew it so well I could forget about it, knowing that the net of her love supported me always. There are no words to say how much I would miss that if it were gone.

"Paula loves you," I said, hoping it was true.

"Not like he did. It's work for Paula."

"You and she are so different," I said. "That makes it harder."

"I can only be me," Shelby whispered. She sounded more like a sad child than a tough customer in leather. "I was happier, milder when he was alive. She didn't like me any better then."

"I'm sorry." I couldn't think of anything else to say.

Shelby threw herself on her bed, her back still to me. "Why don't you go write some postcards?" she said in her tough-customer voice again.

So I went into the sitting room to write a final London postcard to Lily.

Dear Lily,

128   *I saw the guards change at Buckingham Palace*

today. They still looked the same to me. That's a joke. Tell Grady.

Love, Berkeley

I knew these postcards must be frustrating to Lily —Lily with her reporter's mind who always wanted to know what was *really* going on. But I didn't know what was really going on, so how could I tell Lily?

That night we went to see the musical *Les Misérables,* which seemed perfect for the way the trip was going.

At the end, when Jean Valjean dies and his daughter Cosette sings for him, I tried not to cry, but finally I couldn't resist anymore. I stole a sideways look at Shelby and saw her usually stolid face distorted with the effort of holding back tears, and her hands gripped the seat arms as if they were life rafts.

There was a message for me from Spike back at the hotel. I waited until the others had gone to their bedrooms and then called him from the darkened sitting room, waking him up.

"I'm sorry," I said.

"It's okay," he mumbled. "It's okay." He still sounded asleep.

"We're leaving for France tomorrow. Next time I see you, it'll be in Paris."

"Paris," he said.

"I just needed to hear your voice."

"Hi," he said.

"Spike."

"Huh?"

"I miss you."

"Me, too." He yawned. "How's everything going?"

"Bumpy." I wasn't going to howl the way I had the night we'd eaten Indian food. "I'll tell you about it another time. I just wanted to say good night and I love you."

"I love you, too. Hang in there. It won't last forever."

"It seems like it will." No, no, I wasn't going to whine. "I'll be fine. We're doing interesting things."

"Good. That's good. So are we. We can have a my-trip-was-better-than-your-trip competition when we get home."

"I can't wait. You'll win."

"It's not over yet," he said.

Too true.

14

*T*he morning was raw and gray, and the limousine's windshield wipers were the only sound in the car. We rode through the rainy streets on the way to Victoria Station to catch the boat train to France, a long week of togetherness still before us.

At the station, Paula offered around a package of Dramamine while my father fussed with checking luggage and showing our tickets to the attendant. "The crossing could be rough," she said.

Shelby shook her head.

"I never get seasick," my father said proudly, rejoining us and handing Paula a Styrofoam cup of tea.

"It knocks me out," I said. "I only tried it once, in sixth grade, when my class went whale watching. I slept through the whole thing. I'd rather take a chance on getting sick."

"I'm not as brave as you," Paula said, putting two pills in her mouth and washing them down with the tea Ace had brought her. "God, they make their tea so strong. I'm sure it's removed some of the enamel from my teeth."

"Farewell, strong tea," my father said. "Hello, fine wine."

"Farewell, things on toast," Paula added. "Hello, *brioche*."

"Farewell, Tube. Hello, Metro." It was the only difference I could think of.

"Goodbye, shower," Shelby said. "Hello, *douche*."

Her mother gave her a sharp look.

"That's it," my father said, encouraging her. "Farewell to all the wonderful towns we didn't get to see: Upper Piddle and Mousehole, Great Snoring and Catbrain. On to others we won't see: Camembert and Le Mans, Roquefort and Evian."

I couldn't help smiling at my father's high spirits, at the way his nice eyes lit with laughter, at how handsome he looked when he was happy. This was one of the rare times I saw what it was that made Lily, at seventeen, fall for him.

132   Paula linked her arm in his, her new bracelet gleam-

ing in the dull light, and rested her head on his shoulder. He smiled down at her and kissed her forehead. When she closed her eyes, my father traced his finger along her cheek to the corner of her mouth. I felt as if I'd had a peek through an open bedroom door. I looked away.

Once on the train, we found seats arranged so that Shelby and I sat facing Ace and Paula. My father pulled out a French phrase book and began leafing through it as the train pulled away from the station.

"Useful things here," he said. "Listen to this. *Ah-reh-teh-luh! Ohng mah voh-leh!* It means 'Stop that man! I've been robbed!' Hope we won't need that one." He went on and on, getting sillier and sillier, demonstrating his amazing lack of ability to pronounce anything in a way that sounded even vaguely like French: Please bring breakfast to room 702; I'll have the frog's legs sautéed, with no sauce; I'm on the wrong train; I meant to go to Fontainebleau; I must have those shirts done by tonight; will you please remove your hand from my pocket. At least he said that's what he was saying. After every phrase he'd catch my eye, as if daring me to laugh at his efforts to amuse me. It was hard not to, but I didn't.

"Berkeley," Paula said, "I think you're right about this Dramamine. I'm getting awfully sleepy."

"We've got over an hour on the train," my father told her. "Why don't you put your head on my shoulder and get some rest?"

"I don't think I have any choice," she said. "I can hardly keep my eyes open." She leaned against him, closed her eyes, and was instantly asleep.

A young man with an acne-pocked face pushed a trolley down the aisle. "Coffee. Tea. Sandwiches," he intoned dully.

"I'll have a coffee," my father said. "Ladies?"

"A Vittel," I said.

"That's my girl," my father said. "Might as well start drinking French water and get in the right mood. Shelby?" He took out his wallet.

"I'll have a sandwich," she said. "Cheese. And a Coke and a chocolate bar. Make it two chocolate bars. And an orange juice." She had her own money, the correct amount, in the boy's hand before my father could pay for her.

Then we rode in silence, watching the wet green countryside flash by, the little towns, the quick peeps into other people's lives.

When we approached the station at Dover, my father tried to wake Paula. Her eyes showed only the white part and she couldn't hold her head up.

"How many of those pills did she take?" my father asked.

"Two," I said.

"Well, obviously that was too much for her. Paula." He spoke loudly into her face. "Are you okay?"

"Okay," she said in slow motion. "So sleepy."

134

"You've got to get up now. We have to get off the train." He spoke carefully and firmly to her.

She made a couple of sluggish efforts and then fell back into the seat. Gently, my father inserted her arms into her raincoat and tied it around her. He even rearranged the collar of her blouse so it lay straight. "Okay, girls, you get on either side of her and I'll bring the carry-on stuff. We have to get her on the bus to the Hoverport. Don't let her fall down the steps."

Shelby and I supported Paula, her head lolling, down the steps of the train, across a stretch of gravel, almost dragging her, and up the steps onto the bus, with my father pulling her from inside. She slept again for the few minutes' ride to the Hoverport, where, with relief, we deposited her in a chair in the waiting room, her chin on her chest.

"She's going to have a fit when she sees how scuffed up her shoes are from that gravel," Shelby said. "She'll blame it on me."

"I'll tell her it wasn't your fault," I said.

"You will?" Shelby sounded surprised.

"Well, it wasn't. It wasn't anybody's fault. What else could we do? She'd never have made it on her own."

Shelby said nothing. She put her hands in the pockets of her jeans and went to look out at the Hovercraft drawn up on the docking ramp and, beyond it, the gray water peaking and falling. From the look of it, we could all be sorry we hadn't taken Dramamine.

135

At the thought of all of us in Paula's shape, I had to laugh. Shelby turned to look at me and then returned her gaze to the window. I realized that in almost a week together I'd never heard Shelby laugh.

To board the Hovercraft, we had to drag Paula through the rain to another seat, where she sank again into slumber. The noise of the motors inflating the cushion of air underneath the boat was so loud I didn't see how she could go on sleeping, but she did.

The theory that the pillow of air beneath the boat would protect us from the action of the waves turned out to be only that—a theory. In reality, the Hovercraft rose and dipped over the uneven surface of the water, and I was glad I hadn't eaten much breakfast.

"You doing okay?" my father asked. He was between me and Paula, with Shelby on the aisle on the other side of Paula.

"Not bad as long as I don't look out at the horizon going up and down. How about you?"

"I never get seasick," he repeated. Leaning across Paula to Shelby, he said, "You doing okay, Shelby?"

Shelby took the seasickness bag out of the pocket on the chair back in front of her and vomited neatly into it.

"Oh, my God," my father said, blanching.

Granted, it's never a pleasure to watch someone toss their cookies, but I wondered if he would have reacted that way if he'd fathered a child through the normal childhood illnesses and messes. I couldn't reach

Shelby even if there had been something I could do that would be helpful, but I did take a package of tissues from my jacket pocket and pass them down to her.

She wiped her mouth as the stewardess appeared with a cup of water and a fresh seasickness bag. "Don't worry, luv," she said to Shelby. "You aren't the only one. It's a rough crossing today." Then she hurried off to another sick passenger.

Shelby promptly filled the second bag, while my father, looking distinctly less healthy than he had a minute before, reached across Paula and patted her awkwardly on the arm.

Mercifully, the crossing lasted only forty-five minutes, and by the time the Hovercraft rode up onto the beach landing ramp in Boulogne, Shelby was heaved out. The stewardess came along to collect the full bags, and I promised myself that Hovercraft stewardess was one profession I never would aspire to.

We managed to get off the boat, lugging Paula, the carry-on bags, and a haggard Shelby. With our reclaimed luggage, we stood in line at customs, where I felt like a survivor of some calamity at sea.

My father turned to me, his eyebrows raised, and said, "I wonder why they always say getting there is half the fun."

I giggled a little hysterically and my father smiled at me. "You're a trooper, Berkeley. I'm glad you're here."

My giggle stopped. They were words I loved to hear, had longed to hear. But I still couldn't trust them.

When my father brought the rental car to the front of the terminal and came in to get the baggage, Paula roused herself from her seat in the waiting room, staggered to the car, and said, in a slurred voice, "I think I'll drive." She pulled open the nearest door, which fortunately was the passenger side, got in the car, and fell asleep, her head dropping back against the seat.

I looked at Shelby, who appeared to be feeling better now that she was on dry land. We both looked at Paula and then back at each other. Simultaneously we burst into helpless laughter, holding our sides and leaning against the car.

"Oh, stop," Shelby gasped. "My stomach muscles are already sore from so much puking." And then she started laughing all over again.

Ace came out of the terminal with the first load of luggage. "What's so funny?" he asked.

"Paula wants to drive," I said. Then I caught Shelby's eye and we were off again.

"Oh, I'm going to wet my pants," Shelby said, wiping her eyes.

I wondered if this was what happened if you didn't get enough ordinary, everyday laughing; that somehow the need to laugh backed up like a plugged pipe and built to a point where, when it finally burst out, it was excessive and over something that wasn't even that funny.

When we finally calmed down and got into the loaded car, my father handed me a map and said, "We're aiming for Arromanches-les-Bains tonight. See if you can keep me on the right route."

I couldn't even find the town we were in.

My father went roaring out of the parking lot— maybe his driving style was the reason he was called Ace—while I tussled with the map. Luckily we were on the right road, because by the time I finally located us, we could have been miles in the wrong direction.

"Why are we going to Arromanches-les-Bains?" I asked my father. I needed to know how long it would be before we were in Paris, where Spike would be by tomorrow.

"It's close to Omaha Beach, where the Allies landed on D day. I'd like to see that."

Omaha Beach and D day meant nothing to me except that I knew they were connected with World War II. I didn't want to reveal my ignorance to my father, though, so I said nothing.

The countryside already seemed more foreign to me, though it may have been only that I couldn't read the road signs anymore, the way I could in London. I wished I'd paid more attention in French class. I wished I'd practiced with Spike.

We drove for a long time through rolling green hills and towns with stone houses opening right onto the

139

street, their inhabitants walking along smoking and gesturing, carrying long thin loaves of bread under their arms. They looked impossibly alien. My rabbit heart, which had been overpowered for some reason by my lioness in London, awoke with all my old fears of the unfamiliar and the uncontrollable.

"The best butter in the world is supposed to come from these Normandy cows," my father said, gesturing to a pasture where cows stood belly-deep in bright green grass, chewing away. Even the cows seemed different from regular American cows; fuzzier, cuter, more . . . French.

I sank into my corner of the back seat, as if seeking protection from something I couldn't identify.

"I wish we had more time here," my father said, just as I was wishing to be back in San Diego immediately. "There's so much to see, so much we'll be driving right by and don't have time to stop for. Someday I'd like to have weeks to spend here."

"Weeks! How would you manage?" I asked. "You can't speak French."

"I can say *merci* and *omelette*. That should take care of the immediate needs. And I can say 'Take your hand out of my pocket' for anything else." I could see his smile in the rearview mirror.

It seemed so ridiculously inadequate, but he could probably do it just because he thought he could.

140   "How hard can it be?" he went on. "Little kids

speak French over here. Besides, people are people no matter what language they speak. You learn that in sales." He was quiet for a moment, pondering, I imagined, the difficulties of getting around in France. I was wrong.

"Anybody hungry?" he asked suddenly. "I *know* you're empty, Shelby. And I'm starved. Let's stop and get a bite."

He pulled onto the shoulder of the road, in front of a lunch wagon parked on the verge, and got out. "Come on, girls. Your first French meal."

Shelby and I followed him to the lunch wagon. I wished I'd stop expecting to see signs in English, as if the language here was some kind of temporary mistake. Left on my own, I'd probably choose to starve rather than try out my humiliatingly feeble remnants of French. Looking at the menu board, I was surprised to see that I understood some of the words. 'Sandwich,' of course, wasn't much of a puzzle. But I knew that *fromage* was cheese and that *jambon* was ham and that *saucisson* was sausage. *Moutarde* was mustard, and *tomate* I understood, too. The unfamiliar was becoming familiar; maybe there was a way to crack the code of my fears.

"*Bonjour,*" the man in the wagon said, and then added a string of gibberish.

"*Bonjour,*" my father said, expanding his French vocabulary by one word. "American," he said, pointing to his chest. "Hungry." He rubbed his stomach.   141

He might have been communicating with a jungle pygmy.

The man grinned, showing several gold teeth, patted his own stomach, and laughed. He indicated a shelf over his head which displayed cans and bottles, examples of the drinks he had for sale. Then he began opening the covered containers on his cluttered counter, showing us the sandwich fillings and naming them in French. My father tried to repeat the names, and he and the man laughed, more than really seemed necessary, at his pronunciation. Amid great hilarity, we acquired four ham-and-cheese sandwiches and four Cokes. Then my father and the man, again with much laughter, negotiated the payment as Shelby carried the sandwiches and her Coke to the car.

Apparently, communication was communication, no matter how ludicrous it might look to me. I hated the idea that I was learning something I considered valuable from my father.

As we walked to the car, my father and the man waved to each other and called *Au revoir*. The man pointed at me and said, *"Votre fille est très belle."* My father grinned and waved some more, shrugging to indicate he didn't understand, and when we got in the car he tapped the horn twice.

Paula started up in her seat, looked around, asked, "Where are we?" and fell asleep again, her head hitting the seat back with a thump.

142   I had understood what the lunch-wagon man had

said, and of course I liked the idea that he thought I was pretty. And against my will, I liked the idea that he had known that the handsome, charming man who'd executed the purchase of foreign sandwiches with such grace and humor was my father.

15

My map illiteracy caused us to take two wrong turns, which my father insisted were fortuitous adventures, and we didn't reach Arromanches-les-Bains until nearly dark. I was grateful to be reaching it at all.

Paula had finally come to and was making worried noises about finding a decent place to stay. "After all, it is summer," she said. "Vacation season."

"Don't worry, my love," my father said, patting her hand. "Don't I always take care of you?"

Miraculously, he found a parking place on a narrow, twisty street where several inns were located. I followed him into the first one while Paula and Shelby waited in the car. I wanted to see how he could get rooms for us if the clerk didn't speak English.

"*Bonjour,*" he said cheerfully to a woman behind a dark wood counter.

"*Bonjour, monsieur,*" she said. "*Vous voulez des chambres?*"

"*Chambres,*" he repeated. "*Oui.*" He beamed his beautiful smile and held up two fingers. The woman responded to the smile.

"*Deux chambres?*" she asked, smiling back.

He pointed to me and then to himself and held up his two fingers again. "Two *chambres.*"

"*Une chambre pour vous et une pour votre fille?*" the woman asked, trying hard to make things easy for him. She, too, knew we were father and daughter.

They went back and forth, gesturing, smiling, drawing pictures, writing numbers on a piece of paper, until finally they both seemed satisfied with the arrangements. She handed him two keys, each six inches long and looking as if it could open a dungeon, and we went back to the car.

"That was great," I said. I couldn't help it.

"*Merci,* honey," he said. "Nothing to it. Oh, sure, it would be easier if I spoke French. But maybe not so much fun."

He really did think it was fun. Not an opportunity for things to go wrong, the way I did. Could it be that people were born with different genes for the kinds of

145

things they liked or hated? If that was the case, why didn't I seem to have any of his?

My father and Paula had a big room with a view and a sitting room. Shelby and I had a cubicle with the bathroom down the hall. Maybe the language barrier was to blame. Maybe the woman at the desk had liked my father better than she liked me.

After we'd brought in our luggage, the woman at the desk gave us directions to a restaurant around the corner, full of jolly, loud diners and good smells.

"Do you know how to say 'bottle of wine'?" my father asked me as we waited for someone to seat us.

I ransacked my memory banks. *"Bouteille de vin,* I think. I know *vin* is right."

"Splendid," he said, holding up four fingers to the waitress, who smiled at him and did something fluttery with her eyelashes as she led us to a table. All around us, people laughed and smoked and talked so fast I couldn't distinguish a single word. I jumped when the people at the table next to us burst into loud guffaws at the end of a long string of French from a fat man with a beard. At home I'd have heard the joke coming and wouldn't have been so startled. I missed not being able to eavesdrop.

"A *bouteille de vin,*" my father told the waitress. "Vouvray."

"Oui, monsieur," she said, and left.

146   My father beamed. "There's nothing to this. I

bet I could be speaking good French in a month."

"Better wait and see what she brings you," Shelby said, "before you get all excited."

What she brought was a chilled bottle of Vouvray and four glasses. My father threw a pleased glance in Shelby's direction. Shelby refused to meet his eyes. He poured us each a glass of wine and raised his.

"To my family," he said. "Paula, my sleepy darling; Berkeley, my most wonderful creation; and Shelby, my worthy adversary. Come on, Shelby, you have to clink, too. No holding back."

"My father didn't drink," Shelby said, not touching her wine. I'd seen her drink champagne and beer, so I didn't understand where this reluctance was coming from.

"Why, Shelby," Paula said. "You know that isn't so." There was an edge to her voice. "He used to give you a sip of his drink every night. You know how I felt about that."

"It was juice," she said. "Or iced tea."

"I don't know why you're saying that," Paula said. "It isn't true."

"You didn't know what he was like," Shelby said furiously. "I knew him better than you did."

Paula just looked at Shelby with her mouth open. The Dramamine intoxication seemed to have deprived her of some of her lacquered smoothness and self-possession and made her seem more like a regular person who could be confused and confounded.

147

"He was wonderful," Shelby went on. "He was perfect."

"Nobody's perfect," Paula said unevenly. "Don't you remember how he used to tickle you until you couldn't get your breath, and how much you hated that? You'd ask him not to, but he wouldn't listen; he just kept doing it."

"He never did that," Shelby said, leaning across the table.

"When you were afraid of the dark," Paula said, "he wouldn't let me leave a light on in your room, or your door open. He said you were acting like a child and you had to be brave. You *were* a child. I'd stand outside your door listening to you cry and want to kill him."

"Living with you is probably what did kill him," Shelby said through her teeth. "He only wanted what was best for me."

"You know what killed him," Paula said quietly. "Was that best for you?"

"Because of you," Shelby cried, loud enough so that people at other tables turned to look at her. She stood up. "Because of you," she said even louder, and she ran from the restaurant.

Paula half rose, but my father put his hand on her arm. "Let her be alone for a while." He turned to me. "Does she have the room key, Berkeley?"

"We left it at the desk at the hotel," I murmured.

"We'll take her some dinner," he said. "Let's not let her spoil our meal."

"I'm not hungry," Paula said. "Would you mind very much if I went back to the room? I think that Dramamine is still with me."

"Don't try to talk to her," he said. "She can't hear you now." His face was serious and intent.

She looked at him without saying anything and I watched, feeling I'd missed something important that my father seemed to understand better than Paula did.

"Paula," he said.

"All right." She took her purse, kissed him, and left.

Ace poured himself more wine and took a big swallow. "Decided what you want?" he asked me, smiling only with his mouth.

I shook my head and looked at the menu without seeing it. I'd lost my appetite, too.

"Shall I order for you?" he asked gently.

I nodded.

He ordered *poulet normande* for both of us and one to go, for Shelby. While we waited for the food to arrive, he tried to make conversation, but I could tell he was distracted. He was unusually subdued and thoughtful, looking into his wineglass and then up at me. I had an irrational impulse to reach across the table and touch his hand. I curbed it.

Our chicken arrived, sauced in apples and cream and apple brandy, garnished with fresh vegetables and tiny potatoes. I had never tasted anything so good in my life.

149

"Bliss," my father said after his first bite, and gave me one of his real smiles. "Why is it you can hardly get a bad meal in France, or a good one in England?"

"Don't ask me," I said. "But this is wonderful."

"And so are you," he said. "I know that scene with Paula and Shelby was difficult, but you were great."

"Great? I didn't do anything."

"Exactly. And you haven't asked me anything about it, which you have every right to do."

Now I had rights to his personal life? When he'd waited six months to mention to me that he was married?

"It's okay," I said. "I don't want to know."

"But you need to," he said. "They're your family now."

"No," I said too loud. "I mean, they're my step-family, I guess you could call them, but they're not . . . I mean, you're not even . . . I mean, I know you're my father, my biological father, but family is more . . . more . . ." Tears came into my eyes and I put my fork down.

He leaned toward me and put his hand over mine. I let him. "I shouldn't have brought them," he said. "I didn't realize how hard it would be. That's one way I haven't grown up—I still expect happy endings, even happy middles, and I'm always surprised when it isn't that way."

"I could have told you that," I said, my eyes on my

plate.

"I bet you could. We're polar opposites, you and I. I'm always looking for the good part and you're always expecting the worst. Maybe we could teach each other something in between."

I raised and lowered my shoulders fractionally. "Maybe."

"I'm sorry I was such a baby when you were one. I know I've missed a lot."

What about what I'd missed?

"I look at you now and I'm bowled over by the beautiful, exceptional young woman you've become. My daughter."

"I didn't grow up by myself," I said, steeling myself against his flattery. "Don't forget Lily."

"No, of course not. Lily gets a lot of credit. Another beautiful, exceptional person. Too bad I was so ignorant when I was eighteen. Think how different things might have been."

"I wasted too much time wondering about that when I was a little girl."

"I'm sorry, Berkeley. I'm so sorry. But second chances are better than none. Aren't they?"

"It's hard," I said. "I'm still angry."

"I know. And I know the circumstances now aren't ideal. But imagine how well we'd do if they were."

"You're doing it again," I said. "Expecting perfection. There isn't any."

He was silent for a while, still holding my hand. "Do you want to know how Shelby's father died?"

I shook my head but at the same time felt a terrible curiosity. "Okay," I said, and wished I hadn't.

"He killed himself. Shot himself in the head in the living room. Forgive me for being crude, but picture the mess. How much more hostile can a gesture be? This is the man Shelby thinks could do no wrong. And he did drink far too much. His business was on the skids because of it. All he wanted to do was drink and tinker with his hobbies."

I felt light-headed. I heard the judgment in my father's voice, and the scorn—the reactions of a forceful man untempted by another's demon. No wonder Shelby had created her wonderful fantasy daddy. Maybe, with her, he had been someone else.

He sat back in his chair. "It looks as if none of us is destined to get through dinner tonight. You know, it occurs to me that visiting a battlefield and a cemetery tomorrow may not be the best idea I've ever had. I wanted to see this place my father talked so much about, but I think I'd better forget it."

"Your father was here?" I didn't know my grandfather well. I remembered him as a quiet, contained man who had been a widower since I was tiny and who had been in a rest home, suffering from gradually worsening Alzheimer's, for the past seven years.

"He was a corporal on D day. Coming onto that beach, right into all that German gunfire, always seemed as fresh to him as the day it happened. He admitted he was scared white, but I still think it was one of the high points of his life. He certainly never hesitated to take a risk after that. While he still could."

For the first time, I wondered if my father missed his own absent father.

"I'd like to see the beach, too," I heard myself say. Did I think courage could be learned from looking at a place where people had been courageous? "I'll go with you."

"Really?" His delight, and his surprise, were unmistakable, and seemed genuine. "You'd really go with me?"

I nodded.

"That's great. Thank you, honey."

Dear Lily,

Why is it you can hardly get a bad meal in France or a good one in England? This is the kind of question serious travelers ask. I'm starting to feel like one —emphasis on the serious.

Love, Berkeley

16

The next morning, over *café au lait* and croissants in the coffee room of the inn, my father proposed his plan to go to Omaha Beach and the American cemetery. "Nobody has to go who doesn't want to. There's a nice beach here, or shopping, or whatever. I'll be back in a couple of hours to pick up anybody who wants to stay here."

"I'm going," I said.

Shelby, who'd been asleep, or pretending to be, when I came in from dinner, gave me a dark look. "I'll stay."

"I don't think we should leave Shelby alone," Paula said. She flicked a nervous glance at Shelby.

"Even if you stay," Shelby said, "you'll go shopping and I'll go to the beach. Go with them, if you want to." She was as clear as ever in her intention to stay separated from the rest of us.

"There's an invasion museum here in town," Paula said to my father. "I saw a sign for it in the lobby. You could go there."

"I want to see the real place," my father said. "Not pictures."

"Oh, all right," she said, resigned. "I'll go, too."

The road to the bluff above Omaha Beach was rough and narrow and ended in an empty dirt parking lot. At the lot's edge was a map and a sign, in English and French, describing the events of the D-day landing. Cows, grazing on the bluff, rolled their big eyes and, chewing without stop, watched us as we got out of the car and read the sign.

My father began to walk along the bluff top toward a ruined German gun emplacement. "I'll wait in the car," Paula said. "This gives me the creeps."

I followed my father. Peering into the emplacement, I could see how the guns inside would have pointed down onto the broad flat beach—a beach that offered no place to hide.

"How old was your father?" I asked.

"Nineteen." He studied the beach below us.

155

I would be nineteen in sixteen months. I knew I wasn't brave enough right now to get out of a landing craft onto a shore under heavy fire. Could sixteen months make that much difference? And if it wasn't the months that made the difference, what was it?

My father turned away from the bluff's edge, his hands in his pockets, and walked toward the cemetery. I took one last look at the calm silver surface of the Atlantic and the clean white beach at the foot of the bluff and followed.

It could have been a park. There was a great curved white monument with battle maps engraved on it, a long reflecting pool, many green trees. All that spoiled the park-like atmosphere were the rows and rows of thousands of white marble crosses.

Something caught in my chest at the pure and terrible beauty of them.

My father wandered away, down one of the lanes between the crosses. I stayed where I was, reading the inscriptions on the crosses in front of me. So many with the same date of death: June 6, 1944. And with birthdates only eighteen, nineteen, twenty years earlier. Close to my own age. Close to Spike's.

I desperately wanted to be in Paris, where he was.

One cross bore an inscription which read: Here Rests in Honored Glory a Comrade in Arms, Known But to God. The peaceful green and white scene swam in my eyes.

156   I felt so craven and weak, so unforgivably faint-

hearted here. I drew in an embarrassingly loud, shud-dering sob.

My father's arm came around my shoulders and I turned in to him, pressing my face against his shirt, clutching at the fabric and weeping. He held me, stroking my back.

"I know," he said. "I can't imagine what it would have been like, not really, but I can understand why my father's never forgotten."

My father was remembering his own father from another time. It was likely that by now my grandfather *had* forgotten.

"It makes me wonder if I could have done what they did," he said. "Awed, too, that they were able to do it. And, in an odd way, proud of all these men I never knew."

"Yes," I whispered.

"Should I have left you in the car?"

I raised my head. "No. I'm glad I came."

With my father's arm still around me, we walked back toward the parking lot. "I really know how to show a girl a good time," he said. "Seems like one of my ladies is always yelling or crying or throwing up or passing out. You want to wash your face or any-thing?"

In the rest room I put cold water on my face, but my eyes were swollen and red past quick repair. Why couldn't I cry like Mitzi, with sparkling tears and no blotches?

157

Back at the car, Paula sat looking out the window at the cows.

"How was it?" she asked, when my father opened the driver's side door.

"Impressive," he said.

"And Berkeley," she asked. "What did you think?"

I felt too raw to give her the kind of polite answer she was probably expecting. "It was disgusting," I said. "Such waste. And heartbreaking. And inspiring. I'll never forget it." I closed the back door and pressed my forehead against the cool glass.

"Oh," Paula said.

We picked Shelby up in Arromanches-les-Bains and kept going, but not to Paris as I had hoped. Ace wanted to spend the night in Amboise, poised for some châteaux-hopping the next day. All I could think of was Spike. In Paris. With people besides me. With girls besides me.

We checked into the first place we came to in Amboise, the Lion d'Or. The room Shelby and I shared was at the top of the hotel, looking over rooftops to the river. Wide windows stood open, the white eyelet curtains lifting in the breeze off the water. A cat sat on the windowsill, washing its face.

"Bonjour," I said to the cat, scratching its ears. I was willing to try out my French on it, counting on a
158 noncritical audience. *"Parlez-vous anglais?"* I asked

it. Turning to Shelby, I asked, "Have you thought of how lonesome you'd be here if you didn't have anybody to speak English with?"

"It doesn't matter," Shelby said. "It's lonesome anyway."

My heart, which still felt bruised from the Omaha Beach cemetery, responded to the ache in Shelby's voice. "What would make you feel less lonesome?" I asked.

Shelby shrugged. "My father."

Shelby and I and our fantasy fathers—ones we missed when we had them and when we didn't. I picked up the cat and hugged it, then put it into Shelby's lap.

Shelby sat on the bed, her hands at her sides, and watched the cat settle into a soft coil, arranging itself just so. Slowly, she began to stroke the cat with one hand. Even with her head bent over the cat, I could see the tear that fell on the back of her hand.

"I'll be back in a little while," I said, and let myself out the door. I walked through the lobby, past framed pictures of famous French writers and philosophers, and crossed the street to stand at the railing, looking down at the river. I didn't know which river it was, but looking at water always soothed me. That was probably why so many doctors and dentists had aquariums in their waiting rooms.

Since the night before, I was aware of a shift in the atmosphere between my father and me. He seemed 159 more focused on me, more aware, more *there*. I couldn't sustain my anger at him as easily. Was our problem simply that we hadn't spent enough time together? But the question came back to: why hadn't we? He'd explained how he'd changed. I wanted to believe him. At least, I think I did. Without my anger, though, I was lost. I didn't know what to substitute for it.

How much credit should I give him for taking on such a complicated package when he married Paula? Sure, he got a beautiful asset in her, but there was the always difficult Shelby, and the ghost of her father, growing more perfect by the day. Did he really expect that he could eventually win her over by buying her things she didn't want? Couldn't he see what she really needed? But how could he give that to her when she wouldn't take it?

Was I doing the same thing Shelby was, rejecting his sincere overtures for some twisted reason that didn't make much sense? The river flowed on, taking my unanswered questions with it. *Fleuve*, the French word for river, seemed almost a nonsense word, but was the perfect sound for the way the smooth and rolling surface looked, cool and grave and dark, occasional splashes on the surface revealing mysteries hidden beneath.

I went back to the hotel, taking longer to unlock the door to our room than I really needed, giving Shelby 160 plenty of warning of my approach.

She lay on her back, the cat on her chest. She looked as moody as usual.

"Hi," I said. She didn't answer. "Have you ever seen this name of a French writer?" I wrote *Rimbaud* on the pad on the bedside table and showed it to her.

"Maybe," she said, frowning. "Why?"

"You know how it's pronounced in French? I just figured this out from looking at the pictures in the lobby. It's *Rambo.*"

To my surprise, she laughed, making the cat bounce on her chest. We were laughing together when Paula and my father came to collect us for dinner.

I couldn't be sure the memory of the ruined dinner the night before was in everyone's mind, but it was certainly in mine. I made only the most careful, bland conversation and thought, ruefully, that I was starting to sound like Paula. I saw the value of her fluid small talk: it accomplished what silence, Shelby's specialty, could not. There are too many ways to interpret silence.

Back at the hotel, Shelby gave the cat, who had slept on her pillow while we were gone, a napkinful of meat scraps she had saved from her dinner.

"Do you have any pets at home?" I asked, watching her stroke the cat's back while it gobbled down the unexpected treat.

"In Paula's perfect house? You must be joking. Pets shed and smell and have fleas." The cat finished

161

its dinner and began washing itself. After a long silence, Shelby asked, "Do you?"

I was lying on my bed thinking about Spike. I'd almost forgotten what we were talking about. "Two cats," I said. "Madge and Wuffums. They shed and smell and have fleas. But we love them anyway."

"It's funny your father could marry two women who are so different," she said, sounding as if she knew all about Lily just from hearing about our cats.

"Don't forget, he didn't want to stay with me and my mother." I paused. "I used to wish he was dead. I thought it would be easier."

"Don't listen to what Paula says about my father," Shelby said. "I don't know why she says those things. I think she wants to spoil him for me. She can be mean as a snake."

Obviously, even a dead father could still cause trouble.

Shelby curled onto her bed with the cat and was silent. After a while I got up and put on my nightgown. "I suppose we should let the cat out," I said.

"Let's not. It won't hurt if she stays here, will it? We can keep the window open in case she wants to leave."

"Fine with me. Personally, I think a cat on a bed is the perfect decorative accessory."

Shelby gave me a smile that was so young and guileless I did a double take. But by that time it was gone.

The last thing I did before I turned off the light was write to Lily.

Dear Lily,
We went to Omaha Beach today. It made me cry. I think of all they missed, the good things and the bad. It made even my own bad things seem better.
                                        Love, Berkeley

17

On the morning, the cat was still on Shelby's bed. When we were getting dressed, she said, "Someday I'm going to have a hotel for people to come to when they're sad. I'll have cats for them to sleep with and I'll bring them milk and cookies in the afternoon, and I'll always have a fire in the fireplace and books that make them laugh. And lots of hot water for long baths, and soft blankets for them to roll up in and take a nap."

"Aquariums are good, too," I said, brushing my hair, hoping not to scare away this new Shelby. "They're soothing to look at."

"Maybe," Shelby said. "Or maybe I'll have my hotel next to a river. Then I won't have any aquariums to clean."

"Good idea. Cleaning cat boxes can be enough trouble."

Shelby's eyes met mine for the barest moment in the mirror, but in that moment I felt we had really seen each other. Then she ducked her head to hug the cat.

My father had big plans for the day. He had a special château he wanted to show us, one whose history was involved with several special women. I didn't care who they were; what I wanted to do was go straight to Paris and see one special guy. I'd just have to wait.

Chenonceaux was beautiful, with a long gallery built right out into the river Cher on arched piers, an avenue of plane trees, thick and green with summer leaves, leading up to it, and gardens on either side. The small garden belonged to Catherine de Médicis, King Henri II's wife, and the huge garden belonged to Diane de Poitiers, known as the Ever-Beautiful, who was King Henri II's mistress. Catherine got to kick Diane out of the château when Henri died, so having a big garden and being Ever-Beautiful weren't everything. Still, I had to wonder who'd had more fun. My bet was on Diane, although I'm sure Catherine enjoyed the kicking-out part. Major risk-taking might cause you to have a good time for a while, but wasn't there always some price to pay for it? Maybe the good time made the price worth it. That idea was starting to seem more credible to me.

Inside, the château was bright and pretty and elegantly furnished; just big enough to be grand, but small enough to be livable. I felt as if I could get my suitcase from the car and move right in. Of course, there weren't any bathrooms—just the river below to act as a giant sewer—and the grim-looking kitchen downstairs would make baking a cake an unpleasant undertaking. But back in Diane the Ever-Beautiful's time, with plenty of servants, this place must have rung with music and pleasure. Henri levied a tax on every church bell in France and gave her the money for her allowance, so she had plenty to play with. (I couldn't wait to tell Grady this—my own historical factlet.)

I could imagine the high-heeled pumps and colorful skirts of dancers whisking over the black-and-white paving squares in the long gallery over the river. I could picture the light from branches of candles shining onto the water through the rows of windows.

"Wake up, honey," my father said as I stood looking out one of those windows, seeing what wasn't there. "What are you dreaming about?"

"How it would be to live here," I said, still looking out at the river flowing under me, winking in sunlight, not candlelight.

"Drafty and damp most of the year, I'd guess," he

said, purely practical. "But lovely on a summer day like this one." There was romance in his soul, after all.

"Think of all the people who once stood right where I am," I said. "People who had lives, who felt sad and fell in love and had arguments—all the same things we're still doing. And nobody remembers anything about them, unless they left something behind—letters or diaries. It gives me a weird feeling."

The weird part was in thinking about my own life, how vivid and alive all my feelings were—especially about Spike, about my father. To think that one day all that would be gone without an echo was incomprehensible. Why did I bother to agonize over so much when it was only going to vanish into the future?

"A cemetery yesterday and a château full of ghosts today," my father said. "I haven't been a very good tour guide."

I looked out at the water again. "I'm glad I saw them both," I said. What they'd told me was that there was nothing more real than right now; as ephemeral as that was, it was everything.

We collected Paula from the gift shop, where she had apparently bought one of everything, and Shelby from Diane's garden, where she sat sleepily in the sun, and headed for the car just as tour buses full of tourists began to arrive. My father stopped at a *gaufre* stand on the way out and bought us each, except Paula, who watched her figure too closely to snack, a thin, fruit-adorned waffle.

167

"I wish they were called something besides *gaufres*," I said. "I keep thinking of gophers."

"It's the same with mushrooms in Italy," my father said, talking with his mouth full. "Italian for mushrooms is *funghi*. It always makes me think of the stuff that grows in the sliding part of the shower door."

We grinned at each other in a kind of complicity that excluded Paula and Shelby.

When Ace tried to start the car, there was a deafening scraping noise and a cloud of blue smoke from the exhaust, and the transmission wouldn't engage. He got out, slamming the door, and went back to the public phone near the *gaufre* stand to call the car-rental agency. Finally he returned, saying the complications he'd had to go through to make a call on a foreign phone didn't bear repeating, but the upshot was we'd have to make it to Tours to get the car fixed, since it was, after all, summer, according to the barely bilingual person on the phone, and there were no extra cars to exchange it for.

All this meant to me was that we'd be delayed even more in getting to Paris and Spike.

I was right. It took the rest of the day to see to the car. I helped my father, as his pantomimes grew more desperate and elaborate, with the few pertinent words of French I knew, while Paula filed her nails, Shelby leafed through greasy copies of French automotive magazines, and the mechanics looked alternately puzzled and amused at my father and me.

168

The car finally fixed, we struggled through rush hour in Tours. It was still possible to reach Paris in time for a late dinner—until we came to the edge of the city and discovered that we were heading west— away from Paris—instead of east as we'd thought.

"Okay," my father said. "That's it. We're finding a place and putting up for the night. This car is cursed and I refuse to drive it again until tomorrow."

"Will the curse have worn off by then?" Shelby asked.

"Yes," my father said. "Nothing stays cursed forever. Not when I'm the one uncursing it."

With his usual luck, he quickly found a rambling old hotel surrounded by green lawns and brilliant summer flowers. Even the gravel parking lot was laid out prettily.

Once again, Shelby and I had a top-floor room, this time with slanting ceilings, flower-print wallpaper, and the first washcloth I'd seen in France. It came in a cellophane wrapper that declared, in four languages, that it was completely waterproof.

I showed it to Shelby and got another one of her genuine, fourteen-year-old-kid smiles. Then she directed me to the instructions on the back of the door as to what to do in case of fire.

"Have I got this right?" Shelby asked. "*Ne criez pas au feu* means 'Don't yell fire'?"

"That's right."

"Doesn't that seem like poor advice when there's a fire? I wonder what they'd prefer us to yell?"

169

We began speculating. "How about some water up here!"

"Is anyone else as warm as I am!"

"Interesting lighting effects!"

"Who brought the marshmallows!"

Laughing like lunatics, we fell over on our beds. This is what Mitzi and I would have been doing for the whole trip, and it felt wonderful to be doing it with anybody.

At dinner—Ace was right: apparently you couldn't get a bad meal in France—I was too full to order dessert, but my father wanted *crème caramel*.

"Have some, Shelby," he said. "It's my favorite dessert."

"No, thanks," she said. "I'll have the *tarte tatin. Crème caramel* sounds too much like phlegm caramel."

"Shelby," Paula said. "Don't be disgusting."

Shelby shrugged, her tough self again, as if the girl who wanted to run a hotel for sad people and the girl who lay giggling on her bed had never existed.

18

By morning I was frantic to get to Paris. I checked Spike's itinerary for the hundredth time, hoping that this time the dates would be different, that this time I'd find that he had more time in Paris than I'd thought. But the dates remained the same. He'd be in Paris only tonight and the next night and then he'd be heading for the Loire Valley and Normandy, ground I'd already covered. If I didn't see him in the next forty-eight hours, I wouldn't see him until we were both back in San Diego, a time that seemed as far away as Diane the Ever-Beautiful's. Even though I was up early, ready for a rocket start, everyone else slept late. Breakfast was a leisurely affair, while I jiggled impatiently, and then, when I was ready to go upstairs for my suitcase, Paula decided she'd like to sit in the sun by the pool for a while.

"We could stay another night, if you'd like, my love," my father said, standing over Paula's lounge chair and tilting her chin up with his forefinger. "I don't have to be in Paris until tomorrow."

"Oh, no," I said. I was standing beside Shelby's chair, refusing to sit down in the hope that my uprightness would convey how eager I was to hit the road.

"Why? What's the matter?" he asked, looking at me over the tops of his dark glasses.

"Tomorrow night is Spike's last night in Paris." I hadn't wanted to tell him that, but I saw no other way to dynamite him into action. I could only hope he would recognize how important Spike was, without my having to explain any more.

Paula opened her eyes and looked first at me and then at my father. Shelby sat up from her reclining position and paid attention.

"Spike," my father said. "Had you arranged to see him again?"

"We hadn't exactly arranged it. I just thought I would . . . I mean, I'd like to see him. If I can."

"Oh," he said. "I see. In that case, we'd better get moving."

172

I felt a warm rush of gratitude toward him. He understood. The way Lily would have, without an explanation.

"We're only about three hours from Paris."

Every little delay—waiting for Paula to redo her lipstick, waiting while my father worked his combination of charm and smiles and bogus French words on the desk clerk—almost drove me nuts. But finally, finally, we were in the car and on our way. With luck, I'd be having dinner with Spike.

I forgot my father was the lucky one.

As we bombed along the motorway at 130 kilometers per hour, I watched the road signs gradually bringing Paris closer. I hadn't paid attention to the ones for Versailles. My father had.

"Hey," I said, when he took the Versailles turnoff. "I thought we were going to Paris."

"We are, we are. We're only about ten miles away. Relax. I thought we could get a bite of lunch here and have a peek at the palace. We really shouldn't drive by such a monument to French culture. Anyway, I'm sure Spike is out with his group doing things. Even if we got to Paris now, you wouldn't be able to see him."

I wanted to grind my teeth in frustration, even though I knew he was probably right.

We had an interminable, horrifically expensive lunch and then headed for the palace. I should have known when I saw the gigantic cobbled forecourt filled with camera-laden tourists speaking languages I

173

couldn't identify that we weren't going to get away with any "peek."

We saw it all—all the gilded, gorgeous, grotesque excess that represented what the poor French peasants had finally revolted against. I found myself wishing I had a pike of my own—or a musket or a shovel or whatever they'd used—and I knew just who I'd use mine on. My father could hardly have been more arrogant than the Sun King. I believed I'd have an ally in revolution in Shelby, from the way she dragged herself sullenly along, refusing to appreciate anything, even the Hall of Mirrors, which fascinated me in spite of my agitated state.

The palace closed at six and we were still there, only ten miles from Spike. The gardens, unfortunately, were open until dusk, and Ace wanted a peek at those, too.

"Don't you think we should get along to our hotel?" Paula asked. "So Berkeley can call Spike?" I wanted to kiss her.

"Call him from here," he said. I don't know why I hadn't thought of it myself, and the fact that I hadn't made me angrier, for some reason, with my father, who had. Even if Spike wasn't at his hotel, I could leave him a message to wait for me. I could still see him tonight.

I left Ace and Paula ambling through the gardens. Shelby volunteered to go back to the car with me while I got Spike's itinerary out of my suitcase, and then located a pay phone outside a drugstore, where I changed a traveler's check into francs. I wasn't even worried about trying to make a call in French on a French phone. No stupid foreign telephone was going to keep me from Spike.

There was nothing to it. The operator spoke enough English to connect me promptly to Spike's hotel. That's when the problem started. He wasn't there. His whole group wasn't there. They'd never checked in at all.

The clerk, in halting English and with a frenzied attitude, explained that they'd had a reservation which they had canceled three days before. It was possible the trip was canceled. It was possible the group was larger or smaller than originally thought and they had changed to a hotel better suited to that size. It was possible, *pardonnez-moi, mademoiselle*, but it was possible they had met with a mishap; a bus crash, perhaps. He was *désolé*.

I hardly thought they'd cancel their hotel reservation in anticipation of a bus crash. And I wasn't willing to take his flimsy reasoning lying down. In fact, my lioness stood up. The most logical explanation was that they'd had to change hotels for some reason. "Where might they have gone?" I asked firmly. "Aren't there other tourist hotels that specialize in tour groups?"

"*Oui, mademoiselle.*"

"Well, give me those phone numbers. I'll find him that way."

He read me a long list of phone numbers, mixing   175

English and French numbers. I don't know why numbers are so hard to learn in another language, but I had as much trouble with them as he did, and I had to keep dropping more coins into the phone to keep the connection going while we struggled with numerals. Shelby sat on the sidewalk at my feet, forcing pedestrians to detour around her, dividing her attention between me and watching for Paula and Ace to show up at the rental car. I'd expected her to wait in the car and was surprised that she'd accompanied me to the phone and even more surprised that she'd continued to stay with me, at my feet, like some fractious but loyal dog.

I'd called only a few of the other hotels, with no luck, when Paula and Ace came to the car. I wanted even more than I had earlier to take a shovel to my father. If I were in Paris, I could be making these calls from the comfort of a hotel room, instead of from a noisy city street. And I'd probably have had time to find Spike by now.

I explained the situation to them, not bothering to hide my irritation, making sure they knew who I blamed for this state of affairs.

My father tried to placate me with praise. "You've been very resourceful," he said. I already knew that. "We'll find him when we get to our hotel. A few phone calls is all it'll take. They should have left word at the hotel where they were going." Already he was finding a place to lay blame, leading the trail away from himself, justifying himself. My lioness sniffed him out.

She knew what he was going to say next. "Even if we'd gotten into Paris earlier, you still would have had trouble finding him." She was right.

The traffic on the *périphérique* into Paris was beyond anything I'd ever seen, even on L.A. freeways: trucks belching diesel fumes, cars with only inches between them, and everything going at a hundred and twenty kilometers an hour. My father seemed to be enjoying the race.

When we checked into the hotel, another exquisite small jewel of a place, my father asked to have a cellular telephone brought to our room.

"I can help you with the calling, honey. Two of us can find him in half the time."

I didn't want his help: I wanted to find Spike by myself. But it seemed too cranky to decline his offer, even though I was feeling plenty cranky.

I went straight for the phone in our suite, starting my search again. And of course it was my father, with his first call on the portable phone, who located Spike's group. He asked the hotel switchboard to ring Spike's room and then handed the phone to me. I took it into the bathroom and locked the door while I waited for an answer.

"Hello?" It was Spike's voice, breathless as if he'd run to the phone.

"Hi. It's Berkeley."

"Berkeley! Am I glad to hear from you. I've been crazy not knowing where you were. Why didn't we get   177 your dad to give you the name of your hotel here? Then *I* could have called *you*."

"We just got here." I nearly sobbed with relief. "We've been all over France, and then I couldn't find you at the hotel where you were supposed to be and . . ." I took a deep breath.

"It's okay, Berk. You're here now. We just got in from dinner. I'll be right over. Where are you?"

I told him. "And hurry," I added.

19

*M*y father gave me an argument about meeting Spike. "But, Berkeley, we haven't had dinner yet. I wanted your first Parisian meal to be with me." As if dinner could compete with Spike.

Paula gave him one of her eloquent looks and touched his arm lightly with her immaculate hand. He wasn't ready to quit. "Where are you going?" he went on. As if it mattered. As if I cared. "You could get lost."

Paula increased the pressure on his arm. He whipped out his wallet. "Here," he said, thrusting a pile of francs at me. "At least have a decent meal somewhere. Don't let him feed you from one of those carts on the street." As if I'd notice what I ate, as long as it was with Spike.

Is there anything better than reunions, especially ones made difficult to achieve? Being with Spike again, the ease of it, allayed all my old fears that I had been too headlong, too rash in falling for him the way I had, the speed with which it happened. He'd earned the way I felt about him. Love wasn't really like a wave that knocked you over—well, okay, there was some of that—but more like being fed something nourishing, and doing that for someone else. At least the kind of love I wanted was like that.

I couldn't let go of him. We sat in a sidewalk café and I ate soup with my left hand, slopping and dribbling, because I couldn't stop holding his hand with my right.

I gave him a spoonful of my soup. "I want to pour my trip into you like this," I said. "This easily. It's so hard to explain it."

"Things aren't going well?" he asked.

"They are. And then they aren't. Sometimes I feel like my father and I could have fun together. We laugh at the same things and he's so enthusiastic and interested in everything. And sometimes he really seems to be listening to me, tuning in to me. And then he'll do something so selfish—like wasting an afternoon in Versailles when he knew I wanted to get to Paris and he'd said we'd hurry and get here—or so dense, like wanting me to have dinner with him tonight, or so mean, like buying Shelby a sweater that's so unlike her it's clear he hasn't paid the slightest bit of attention to what she's really like . . . I just can't figure him out. It's like there are four or five personalities wrestling around inside him and none of them ever wins."

"But you like one of his personalities?"

"I love one of them. And I can forgive that one, and understand why he did what he did to me. But the others, the other parts of him—I can't stand them."

"He sounds complicated."

"Complicated and confusing. I don't want him to be that way."

"But that's how he is," Spike said.

I'd kept waiting for the "real" father, the one I wanted, to emerge from the disguises I thought Ace wore. It was the same way I'd waited for the temporary mistake of the French language to quit being spoken in France and the "real" language of English to show up. But I realized I'd been getting used to French, recognized that this language was what was real here.

Shelby and I and our fantasy fathers. She let her pain over her loss show more than I ever had, but that was our main difference; otherwise, we both yearned for what didn't exist. But because her father was dead, she could make him into anything she wanted and, unlike Ace, he wouldn't contradict her with his every-day actions.

Ace. Maybe I could learn to call him that, to distinguish him from the father I wanted, the one I could have called Daddy.

"I don't even know what a father's for," I said.

"He's one more person to love you," Spike said. "To help you, to play with you, to depend on."

I put my spoon down, giving up on the messy business of trying to eat. Suddenly I wasn't hungry anyway.

I got back late to the hotel, but Shelby was still up, sitting cross-legged on her Louis XIV reproduction bed, watching a dubbed episode of *Dynasty* with distractingly unsynchronized lip movements.

"Hi," she said. "How's your main squeeze?"

"He's fine."

"Man, this TV is weird. All kinds of reruns of American shows—*Dallas, L.A. Law, Cheers*—with bad lip-synching, and variety shows with Elvis impersonators singing in French and Michael Jackson impersonators singing in phonetic English that's impossible to understand."

"Why are you watching it, then?"

"I'm so bored my teeth hurt. You won't believe the dinner I had to eat. It took hours and was full of things that we'd throw away at home—cow innards and weeds and stuff, all done up to look like works of art. And it cost a fortune. What a scam."

"I had onion soup. It was good."

"You had the right idea. You should have heard

him go on about whether old hunk-o'-burning-love Spike was a good idea for you. You're young, you know. Too young to be having such an intense, exclusive relationship."

I turned from hanging up my clothes, indignant. "And what was he doing when he was my age? Getting a girl pregnant and having to be dragged into marrying her. Please."

"Yeah? I wonder what all his worshippers would think about that."

"His what?"

"You know—the people who come from all over the world, who say they've learned English just for the privilege of listening to him talk about himself."

"What do you mean?"

"His How-to-Get-Everything-You-Want-from-Life seminars. What he's doing in London and here. Why we had to come on this stupid trip."

"My father sells life insurance," I said.

"Not anymore. Where have you been? You didn't notice when he changed careers?"

"How could I notice when I hardly ever saw him?" I sat down on the bed. "Tell me."

She used the remote control to mute the television. *Dynasty* made as much sense without the sound as it did with it. "He sold insurance. He sold a lot of insurance. He got so good at it that his company asked him to run some seminars for the other salesmen on how to do it as well as he did, as if such a thing was

183

possible. Then he started broadening his seminars into more than insurance, into life. Then he formed his own company: Take Charge, Inc. And he's making a fortune telling other people how to get everything they want. How do you feel, being part of his own personal example of taking charge?"

"Me?"

"When a guy like him wants something, how can you resist? And he wants you, folded into his brand-new family."

"Is that why he invited me on this trip? To be a case study in his seminars?" That would certainly explain his performance in the airport in Los Angeles; how much he needed me.

She shrugged. "I've had my suspicions that's why he keeps after me. What a satisfying story that would make—Resistant Rebellious Stepdaughter Won Over by Irresistibly Persistent Take-Charge Guy."

I wouldn't believe it. The man who'd comforted me at the Omaha Beach cemetery, who'd seemed to understand just what I was feeling, couldn't be using me. It could not be true. But the idea of it kept me awake well into the night.

My postcard to Lily that night read:

Dear Lily,
We went to Versailles today. The peasants had the right idea, killing off all those arrogant nobles who were only interested in indulging themselves.
Love, Berkeley

The next morning, over breakfast, I said to my father, "I didn't know you taught these seminars. How come you never mentioned it to me?"

"I never did?" he said, looking surprised. "I must have."

"No," I said. "I thought you still sold insurance."

"I guess I didn't think about talking shop with a child. And you never asked me about my work."

"I was supposed to ask, 'So, have you changed careers lately?' " I could feel the pressure of old rage in my chest and I didn't care that Paula and Shelby were listening.

He put down the knife he was buttering his croissant with and took my hand. "Of course not. I'm sorry. What would you like to know about my work? I haven't a lot of time right now—in fact, I have a seminar to run shortly—but we can get a start on any questions you have."

Could I ask if I was an experiment for his take-charge method? Could I ask if he really wanted me there at all? Could I ask if he really loved me at all?

No, I couldn't. "Does taking charge always work?" I asked finally.

"That's what I say in my seminars. When it doesn't, it's because you didn't try hard enough, your goals weren't clearly enough defined, or some act of God intervened. There you have it, the capsule summary of a whole day's program." He smiled confidently. "It's always worked that way for me."

"But wouldn't you say, Ace," Paula interjected,   185

"that sometimes you have to adjust your goals, that sometimes you can't achieve exactly what you're aiming for?"

She seemed to have something specific in mind, but I didn't know what; something to do with her marriage to him perhaps. Or with her first marriage. Or with Shelby. Or me?

"You're absolutely right, my darling. That's what I call defining your goals more clearly."

He rose, taking a last swallow of coffee and patting his lips with his napkin. "I've got to go. I'll see you in time for dinner tonight."

"I have a date with Spike," I said.

"But, Berkeley." He gave me a wounded look. "We have to have *our* special dinner."

"I didn't know there was one."

"This is Paris. The finest cuisine in the world is here. I want to share it with you."

This was the first I'd heard that Parisian cuisine was his to share. As far as its being the finest in the world, I'd a lot rather have had a *carne asada* burrito in San Diego than cow innards and weeds in Paris.

"Spike leaves tomorrow," I said. "We can do it tomorrow night."

"I'm very disappointed," he said, picking up his briefcase and kissing Paula absentmindedly. "But that will have to do. I've got to go." And he did.

"Anybody interested in wandering around with me?" Paula asked brightly in the silence that followed his departure. "This is such an interesting neighborhood, all the shops and galleries. I'd rather just poke through them than do the regular tourist things."

Shelby and I looked at each other. "Sure," Shelby said, astonishing me, and Paula, too, from the look on her face. "With one condition."

"What?" Paula asked.

"No fancy lunch. I want a sandwich and an Orangina from a street vendor."

"Fine," Paula said. "No problem at all with that." She sounded delighted.

"I don't want to sit in some stuffy place trying to find something to eat that's not a mollusk or a root."

Paula grinned. "Fine, fine. I'll go have my bath and get dressed."

The narrow streets of the Left Bank were full of shops and restaurants, galleries and decorators' offices, hairdressers and markets. People who looked like students, the young men in leather pants and earrings, the young women in skimpy outfits and interesting haircuts, sat at sidewalk cafés drinking tiny cups of very black coffee and smoking and arguing seriously and self-consciously.

Shelby made us stop in a tiny lingerie shop to see if French underwear was as naughty as she'd heard. Gamely, Paula went in and refrained from commenting on the wispy garments with holes in critical places. They didn't look any naughtier to me than the stuff at

187

Frederick's of Hollywood and they were a lot more expensive. We didn't buy anything, though I would have gotten something for Mitzi if the prices had been lower. She'd have loved the idea of underwear straight from France.

"Oh, look at these scarves," Paula said as we passed a row of street carts selling magazines, jewelry, scarves, food. She removed one from the display and threw it around her shoulders. "Oh, you have to have one of these, Berkeley. You could wear it on your date tonight, the way the Parisiennes do. They look so chic."

Even in my dreams I'd never be chic, but I could imagine what the scarf with the big pink roses would look like over the white dress I planned to wear that night. I searched for the price tag.

Paula pulled the scarf from the rack and put it around me. "It's my treat," she said. "You have to have it. It's perfect on you." She was right. I gave in without a struggle. "How about you, Shelby," she asked. "Is there one you'd like?"

To the surprise, I'm sure, of both Paula and me, Shelby put her hand, with no hesitation, on a black-and-white paisley.

"It's lovely," Paula said. "A good choice."

Her mother's approval brought a little scowl to Shelby's face, but she didn't retreat.

"Don't you want one?" I asked Paula.

"I haven't seen one I can't live without. Anyway,

it's more fun to buy them for you girls. Especially when one of you has such a big date tonight."

While Paula paid for the scarves, Shelby moved to the next cart, where she bought, with her own money, a big silver Celtic cross on a leather thong which she immediately hung around her neck. One gift from her mother was apparently all she could tolerate.

Paula joined her at the cart. She ended up buying a silver bracelet for herself and a pair of dangly pink quartz earrings which she gave to me. "They'll look so pretty with your scarf," she said. Again, I took what she bought me. I believed her gift-giving came from a generous spirit and a personality that simply loved to shop, unlike my father's, which seemed to have invisible strings and hidden meanings and made me suspicious and hesitant. It didn't escape me that Shelby was as suspicious of Paula's motives for buying her presents as I was of Ace's buying them for me. And maybe she was right. Our parents could be different with their own children than with someone else's.

We had our sandwiches and our Oranginas and wandered through the afternoon, not buying anything more, stopping once for ice cream, once for coffee. Some French magic had descended on us, giving us all another gift, that of the most casual, relaxed hours I'd experienced on the whole trip.

"Okay if I sit in here while you get dressed?" Paula asked me when I came out of the bathroom wrapped

189

in one of the hotel's terry-cloth robes and found her sitting on my bed. Shelby lay on her bed, reading a science-fiction novel.

"Sure," I said, although I admit I was startled to see her. Lily sometimes sat with me while I got ready to go somewhere and I usually liked it, unless I got the idea that she was there to instruct me about something. I didn't have that feeling about Paula's presence. I took it to mean that she'd enjoyed the time we'd spent together, the three of us, that afternoon, and wanted more of it.

"Why don't you leave your hair pinned up like that?" she asked. "Those ringlets around your face look sweet."

I looked in the mirror. "Don't you think it looks like I just got out of the bathtub?"

"I can help you fix it. Will you let me try?"

"If you promise you won't get your feelings hurt if I don't like it."

"Sure. Sit down."

I had to admit I liked my new tousled do. It made me somebody else, somebody almost like me, but a little foreign. A little chic. And my new pink earrings showed more with my hair up. "I like it," I said, turning my head for a better mirror view. "But I look like somebody else."

Paula arranged a curl in front of my ear. "You are somebody else. Don't think the days of this trip haven't changed you."

I wondered if Paula was as perceptive about herself, about why she was with Ace, about why Shelby was being so difficult, as she was about me. I would put money on it.

"I'll wait outside while you finish dressing," she said. "I think Spike's going to like what he sees."

When she'd gone, Shelby spoke for the first time. "I thought you didn't like dangly earrings."

"And I thought you didn't like my PTA president look," I said, still admiring myself in the mirror.

"She's been dying for somebody to make over into her image."

At the angry tone of Shelby's voice, I turned to her. "I don't think that's what she was doing. Anyway, what were you trying to do the night we went dancing in Camden Town?"

"That was different."

"Really? How? Because it's how *you* thought I should look? You know, you and Paula are more alike in some ways than you want to think."

"Just the way you and Ace the Magnificent are," she retorted, not looking at me.

"What do you mean by that?"

"You can both get whatever you want. On top of everything else, now you've got my mother."

I was speechless, while Shelby glared at her book. Finally I said, "You know I don't have everything I want. And you could have her. She'd rather have you than me any day."

191

"She wants me her way, not my way."

"You don't make it easy. I have no idea what went on in your house, but how do you think she feels when you accuse her in public of being responsible for her husband's death?"

Shelby sat up, yelling, "Don't you dare talk about my father. She made him miserable. It *was* her fault."

"He could have left her," I said. "It's not such a hard thing to do. My father did it. And if he'd left Paula, he could have stayed in touch with you." I didn't know that, but I wanted to think it was so.

"So why did he die?" Her face was red and the biggest tears I'd ever seen splashed from her eyes.

I sat on her bed and she turned away from me. "It had nothing to do with you. It was something, I don't know what, but it was something with him. He loved you and he was flawed, that's all. You can remember the good things about him even if Paula doesn't. You don't have to be unhappy because he was."

She put her arms around my waist and her face in my lap and wept into the terry-cloth robe. I stroked the tangled mess of her hair while I said goodbye to some fantasies, and I hoped she did, too.

Paula knocked on the door. "Spike's here," she called.

Shelby flopped away from me, burying her face in her pillow. "Go on," she said in a muffled voice. "Get dressed."

192   I hurried into my dress, my bee necklace, my scarf.

My reflection in the mirror showed flushed cheeks and glistening eyes. Apparently, strong emotions were a good cosmetic.

As I put my hand on the doorknob to leave, Shelby said, from her pillow, "Have a good time. A really good time."

20

On the elevator Spike took my hand. "You look terrific," he said. "And . . . I don't know . . . different."

"It's my hair."

"It's more than that, but I don't know what."

"Maybe," I said. "Where are we going?"

"For a boat ride on the Seine. It's the farewell-to-Paris party for my group. You'll like them. And, lucky for you, there aren't any girls who are good whistlers."

I did like them, and what could be more romantic

than a boat trip on the Seine on a warm French evening with my main man. I'll tell you: nothing.

"What time do you leave tomorrow?" I asked Spike on the way back to my hotel after the boat had docked. It was midnight, but because it was still so warm, the streets were full of strollers and dog walkers and every seat at the sidewalk cafés was taken.

"Early. Bags out at six. Breakfast at seven. On the bus at eight. At Versailles by nine. It never works out that neatly, but sometimes we get close." His arm was around my shoulders and he pulled me closer to him.

"I don't want to spoil your impression of Versailles by telling you I thought it was ostentatious beyond belief and that I don't blame the peasants for revolting against such self-indulgent extravagance."

"Oh, thanks. I always like to make up my own mind. What are you doing tomorrow?"

"I don't know. And I don't care. I'm just glad to be one day closer to going home."

"I thought you and Shelby might be doing better from what you told me about tonight."

"I can't tell. Sometimes it seems that way and other times not. I'm not even sure if I like her, but I'm interested in her, if you understand the difference."

"Yeah, I do. I felt that way about her, too. Like I wanted to get a can opener and see what was going on inside."

"I'd like to do that with my father. Especially since I found out about Take Charge, Inc."

195

"Just because he does those seminars doesn't mean he's using you, you know. Why can't you believe he's finally ready to make a connection with you, no matter what he does for a living?"

"He doesn't seem to know how to make connections."

"Sure he does. He's married. He has colleagues. He just makes different kind of connections than you do. You like them deep and involved and mutual, don't you?"

"They're better that way." I stood at the bridge railing, looking down at the reflections of lights swimming on the dark river. "Why doesn't he see that?"

"Who knows. He's afraid? He's incapable? He's shallow? He's not interested? It's too much trouble? It's him, not you. How many times do I have to tell you?"

I'd said the same thing to Shelby. Lily had said the same thing to me. Why did it still seem like news?

Spike stood behind me, his arms around my waist. He already knew more about love—the kind of love I wanted—than Ace ever would.

"He doesn't ask me anything about myself," I said, my voice trembling.

Spike tightened his arms around me. "He's missing a lot."

I rested my head on his chest and took a deep breath. "I love you," I said.

196   "Well," he said, turning me around in his arms, "in

that case, why don't we go have an espresso and post-pone taking you back to the hotel. The night is but a kitten."

Sitting outdoors on a dulcet Parisian night over tiny cups of strong bitter coffee that neither of us really liked, I thought that, no matter what else happened to me in all my life, this was one of the moments I would remember when I was an old, old lady.

"I wish you were going with me tomorrow," Spike said as we neared my hotel, walking more and more slowly the closer we got.

"Don't tempt me," I said. "Did you know that King Henri II taxed all the church bells in France to make an allowance for his lover Diane de Poitiers, the Ever-Beautiful?"

"Of course not."

"Impress somebody with that fact before I see you again."

"I'd tax all the church bells for you if I could."

I was afraid I was going to cry. "I want to be home," I said. "I want us to be getting off work and going to your house to cook vegetables and watch movies. I want my real life back."

Spike lifted his face to the star-spattered sky. "I'm looking for that lightning bolt that's going to strike you. This is *Paris*! Do you know how many people would love to be here?"

"I know. I'm an ungrateful wretch."

"Yes, you are. But I don't care." He stepped into 197

the doorway of a shuttered antique shop, pulling me to him, kissing me. "I thought it would be unseemly to do this in the lobby of your hotel."

"This is Paris, as you keep reminding me. I think it's okay just about anywhere."

We kissed again. "I'll see you next in San Diego," he said. "In a week and a half, that's all. I'll call you the minute I'm home and you can come over and watch me sleep off my jet lag while you gloat because you're already over yours."

"I'm not supposed to have any. My father says he knows how to avoid it, but I must have done something wrong because I had it anyway when we got to London."

"He was trying to impress you. We men often make dopes of ourselves and say dumb things trying to impress pretty girls."

My father had been trying to impress me, I knew that much. What I didn't know was why.

Finally I had to say good night to Spike one last time and go in to write my postcard to Lily.

Dear Lily,
I went boating on the Seine tonight with Spike. I wish we'd been on San Diego Bay.
                              Love, Berkeley

I slept heavily, and even the sound of the phone ringing in the sitting room barely penetrated my dreams. Staying asleep until it was time to go home seemed like a good idea.

I was finally awakened at nine by my father dropping onto the side of my bed and saying, "Up, my darling. Paris awaits. I have nothing on until this afternoon, so you and I can do the town this morning. The birds are singing, the sun is shining, and the air is like champagne. Let's go have some."

I pulled my head out from under the covers and looked around me. Shelby's bed was empty.

"I'm sleepy," I said.

"Nonsense. You can sleep at home. You can sleep when you're old. Sleeping is a waste of time now." He stood up. "Your *café au lait* is in the sitting room getting cold. We're going to the Louvre. Every living person should see the Winged Victory of Samothrace and the Maximilian Tapestries at least once." He closed the door behind him as he left.

I lay on my back, staring at the ceiling, thinking that most of the world, including me, had never heard of the Winged Victory of Samothrace and the Maximilian Tapestries and would never know what they'd missed. I sighed and got up.

Shelby was watching French news on TV while Paula drank coffee and looked through a guide to shopping in Paris. News in French sounded quaint and trivial. I liked not being able to understand it.

Paula looked up when I came into the room. "Good morning," she said. "Have a good time last night?"

"A great time. Spike liked my hair."

"I'm glad." She returned to her guidebook.

My father came briskly out of his bedroom. "Good," he said when he saw me. "Eat, eat. We've got places to go. I'll make a few calls while you finish." He went back into the bedroom.

Fifteen minutes later, he was ready to go. "Leave it," he said to me. "I'll buy you a big expensive lunch on the Champs-Elysées."

"Isn't anybody else coming?" I asked.

"Paula's going shopping and Shelby has mysterious business of her own to pursue. So we'll be reunited at dinnertime. *Allons.* That means let's go. I'm getting better at French every day," he said smugly.

We saw the Winged Victory of Samothrace and the Maximilian Tapestries and a lot of other wonders, and if there's such a thing as indigestion from too much sumptuous art, that's what I got. After this and the British Museum, I would never again think of museums as dusty, boring places.

"Great art should be taken in small bites," Ace said, leading me away from the Louvre after we'd barely made a dent in it. We strolled through the Carrousel Arch into the Tuileries. The gardens were dry and dusty, but the air was heavy and sweet with perfumes released from the flowers by the morning heat. Children's sailboats filled the ornamental ponds and vendors sold ice cream and popcorn and wind-up flying birds that looked real. On one of the public benches a woman sat on a man's lap and they kissed with an astonishing lack of restraint.

I thought of Spike, at Versailles now, and missed him sharply.

Somehow we managed to cross through the lethal traffic of the Place de la Concorde and made our way along the Champs-Elysées. The gardens beside the sidewalk were full of oblivious lovers on benches, on the grass, leaning against trees. My father's hand on my elbow was warm and I was grateful for it.

We passed women with shaved heads and see-through blouses, elegantly dressed ladies with multiple poodles on leashes, men in business suits, men wearing makeup and earrings. It was a moving circus.

We made the turn at the colossal Arc de Triomphe at the end of the boulevard and headed back down the Champs-Elysées on the other side of the avenue. I might never be a Master of the Universe like Ace, but I'd learned to enjoy the strangeness, the mystery of a foreign place.

"Hungry?" my father asked. "Had enough of the show?"

"No," I said. "I mean, I'm hungry, but I'd like to sit outside so I don't miss any of the show."

With his customary luck, we got an outside table in the shade at a restaurant separated from the sidewalk by a wrought-iron railing and a striped awning.

"This all right?" he asked.

I nodded, looking at the menu. "What's a *croque monsieur*?" I asked him.

"A ham-and-cheese sandwich dipped in batter and fried. It's good. You'd like it."

"And what's a *croque madame*?"

"You mean you can't tell the difference between a *monsieur* and a *madame*?" he asked in a teasing tone. "It's the same as a *croque monsieur* except it has an egg on the top." He wiggled his eyebrows. "Oh, those French."

I made a face. "I'll have the onion soup," I told the waiter.

"And I'll have the *croque monsieur*," Ace said. When the waiter left, he said, "I enjoyed this morning, seeing your reactions to the art, the people. Your face is so expressive. I can always tell what you're thinking."

He didn't have a clue what I was thinking.

"I'm glad you didn't spend this morning with Spike," he went on.

"With Spike? How could I? His group left this morning."

"Didn't you get the message? He called this morning while you were still asleep. Something was wrong with their bus and they had to stay in Paris until this afternoon."

For the first time, I understood what people meant when they said they were so angry they saw red. An actual red haze swam before my eyes. "Who was supposed to give me this message?" I asked him tightly.

"I wrote it on the pad by the phone. I thought you'd see it." He looked so innocent, so bewildered.

"Why would I look there unless somebody told me to?" If he'd really been able to read my thoughts, he would have been on his way out of town. "Who do you think I'd rather have been with this morning? That's why you didn't tell me. Admit it." I stood up.

"Berkeley, please, sit down," he said. "It was a mistake, an oversight. I got busy with my calls. I forgot."

"I don't believe you," I said. "You forgot the same way you forgot to tell me Paula and Shelby were coming on this trip with us. Don't you know what a lie is? I'm not just some project for Take Charge, Inc."

"Of course you're not. But you're my daughter. This trip was supposed to be for us."

"And Paula and Shelby, too, don't forget them. You should have told me!"

I climbed over the thigh-high railing beside our table and ran down the Champs-Elysées, back toward the Louvre.

"Berkeley!" I heard my father's voice behind me, and I ran faster.

"Berkeley, wait!" His voice was fainter, but I didn't turn to look back. I was so blinded by tears I wouldn't have been able to see him anyway.

21

I ran into the park and dropped onto a bench set back from the sidewalk, put my face into my hands and wept. I could have had Spike to cry to if it weren't for my arrogant, manipulative, know-it-all father.

I hated him. I didn't care if I never saw him again in my life.

When I finally stopped crying and caught my breath, I was starving. I bought a bag of popcorn from a vendor in the park and found a public phone to call Spike's hotel, in case he was still there.

Spike's group was gone. The bus must have gotten fixed.

Going back to our hotel was the last thing I wanted to do, so I wandered up a side street, not even noticing the name of it. I wished I could walk all the way to San Diego.

When I got tired, I stopped at a café and had a cup of tea and a sandwich. I ordered it in French.

I wandered more after I'd eaten. For some reason, I wasn't worried about getting lost. I'd find my way back, somehow, when I had to.

I bought some stylish patterned socks for Mitzi. Then I bought another pair for myself, and some for Lily and some for Nell. They were great socks and I wanted us all to have them. Paula wouldn't wear such socks on a bet. Maybe Shelby would. I bought another pair for her. I used up the francs my father had given me.

I went into a hotel next to the sock shop and changed the pounds he had given me in London into francs. He owed me more than he could ever make in money.

I bought a belt for Grady. It had a silver buckle shaped like an *escargot*. He would laugh and love it and wear it. Ace wouldn't wear it if it was the only belt he owned.

A clock bonging six surprised me. I supposed I should head back. At least I was one afternoon closer to going home.

By taking my time, concentrating, convincing myself I could do it, I deciphered the map at the entrance 205 to the Métro. I'd have to change trains once to get back to the hotel, but I knew I could do it. It was something that could be learned, like driving a car. Like tying your shoelaces. Like speaking French.

As I was getting out of the elevator directly across from our suite, the door flew open and Paula rushed out. When she saw me she dropped her purse, threw her arms around me, and then stepped back, holding me at arm's length.

"Oh, thank God," she said. "Where on earth have you been? We've been worried sick, and I was afraid your poor father would lose his mind."

"You didn't worry when Shelby was this late getting back to the hotel in London," I said, unreasonably calm.

"Oh, Shelby," she said with a wave of her hand. "She does that all the time. I always say I'll wait twenty-four hours before I call the police and I've never had to yet. But that's not your style. You wouldn't stay away unless something was wrong."

"Something was," I said.

She looked at me narrowly. "Are you all right?"

I nodded.

"Well, what are we doing standing out here in the hall? We've got to let your father know you're all right so he can get off the phone and stop yelling at the Préfecture of Police to launch a city-wide search." She bent and picked up her purse.

"Is that what he's doing?"

"Well, of course. What did you think he'd be doing after his daughter disappeared?"

"Did he tell you what happened?"

"Only that, without warning, you ran off from where the two of you were having lunch."

I reached behind Paula and shut the door to the suite, leaving us out in the hall. "That's not entirely what happened. He lied to me about something—he knew what he'd done—and I left the restaurant."

Paula looked at me, her flawless face unchanged, and I realized she wasn't surprised by what she'd heard.

"It wasn't exactly a lie, I'm sure he'd say," I went on. "He just 'forgot' to tell me something. The same way he didn't tell me you and Shelby were coming on this trip with us."

Paula said, "I wondered. He does that."

"How can you stand it? How can you ever know if he's being straight with you?"

"He could have worse habits. Believe me, I know what it's like to live with someone with those. He only does it to have his own way—and he thinks his way is the way that will make everybody happiest. That's better than somebody who doesn't care what makes somebody else happy, who only wants his way for selfish reasons. Your father is a very generous and attentive man. That makes it easy for me to overlook his faults. Doesn't it count for something with you?"

What must Paula's marriage to that perfect father

of Shelby's have been like if my father's deviousness and manipulation looked good to her?

"I went seventeen years with very little of his generosity and attentiveness," I said. "And being lied to is not the kind of attention I want. His way isn't what makes me happiest."

"He's a good man, Berkeley," Paula said. "And he loves you. He canceled his seminar this afternoon to search for you."

"He wouldn't have had to if he'd told me the truth," I said. "Well, we might as well go relieve his mind."

Paula dug in her purse for the suite key and opened the door. "Ace," she called, "Berkeley's back."

My father came out of the bedroom. His hair was rumpled and his tie hung loose and crooked. He ran to me and hugged me tight while I stood passively, my arms at my sides. Over his shoulder, I could see Shelby watching TV. She raised her hand and twiddled her fingers at me in greeting.

"Oh, my God, are you all right?" Ace asked and, without waiting for an answer, went on, "I've been beside myself. I've been on the phone all afternoon. I've offered a reward. I canceled all my appointments. You worried me so."

So it was all my fault he was worried. Had he forgotten how it happened that I left? Or did he really not understand why I had been so upset?

Shelby turned toward us again and this time looked quite interested.

My father laughed a little and ran his hand through his hair. "I'd better call Inspector Lenoir and let him know you're all right." He disappeared into his bedroom.

I went into my own bedroom and a minute later Shelby came in. She closed the door and leaned back against it.

I threw the plastic bag of socks and Grady's belt on my bed.

"You went shopping?" Shelby asked.

"Yes. For my mother and my friends. And for you." I found her socks and handed them to her.

"Cool," she said. "Thanks.

"He can drive you nuts," she went on, pulling off her boots and putting on the socks. She lay on her back, her feet in the air, admiring the new socks. "And then make it be your own fault. I've learned a lot from him."

"I think I have, too," I said, sitting down on my bed. "I'm just not sure what all of it is yet."

"You're lucky you're going away to college in the fall."

"You know where I'm going? UCLA."

Shelby made a sound between a laugh and a snort. "Great. You can come over for dinner a lot."

I groaned and lay down, my hands behind my head.

"You know where I want to go to college?" Shelby asked. "Middlebury. It's in Vermont. As far away from L.A. as I can get. I'm going to major in creative writing and languages. I'm going to travel everywhere and write about what happens."

"Will you write about him?"

"Of course. Him and Paula. And my father. You, too."

"Leave me out of it."

"I can't. You're in it now."

"What will you say about him?" I asked.

"I don't know. I'm not finished thinking about him yet. The hardest part to explain will be how wonderful I sometimes think he is and how I have to make myself resist that."

"Why can't you think he's wonderful and at the same time know what his weaknesses are?" I asked Shelby. Asked myself.

"That may be possible," she said. "But not yet."

"Not all weaknesses are equal, are they?" I asked. "And what's acceptable to someone else might not be acceptable to you."

"That's something I learned from him," Shelby said. "It also depends on how much there is to compensate for the weaknesses. I learned that from my father."

At dinner we might as well have sat at two different tables. Shelby and I were silent. Ace ordered champagne to celebrate my return, but I found it impossible and fraudulent to join in the toast. Paula did her small-talk trick and, once again, she covered up most of the silences, but the effort must have been considerable.

When we returned to the suite, Paula went directly to her room. I could sympathize—all that chitchat must be depleting. Shelby, too, disappeared without a word to anyone. I paused in the sitting room to pick up a guidebook. I planned to see Paris tomorrow, and to see it by myself. After tonight there'd be only one more full day before we went home, and I wanted the time to pass as quickly and as easily as possible.

As I turned to my bedroom I saw my father standing quietly, waiting for me. He held his hand out to me and said, "Berkeley. Please talk to me."

"Good night," I said.

Shelby was in the bathroom, the shower water running. I knew I'd never again yearn for my father. I'd satisfied my need for him, though not for some other father, one who'd have to remain a fantasy. I wondered if Ace hurt as much as I did at the way things had turned out.

The most painful part was that sometimes he *was* the wonderful, strong, adorable, and adoring Daddy of my finest fantasies. But not often enough.

When Shelby came out of the bathroom, I was writing my last postcard to Lily.

Dear Mom,

I went to the Louvre today. I'm ready to come home, Mom.

Love, Berkeley   211

22

He was gone by the time Shelby and I woke the next morning, making up for his canceled obligations of the day before, and Paula was about to leave on a tour of antique shops with a hired guide.

After she left, Shelby asked me, "What are you going to do today?"

"I'm going to see Paris. We'll be leaving tomorrow—"

"Not a moment too soon—"

I grinned at Shelby. "Not a moment too soon—and I've hardly seen anything." Impulsively, I added, "Want to come?"

"You sure?"

"As long as you want to see what I want to see. If not, we can head in different directions." I didn't intend to accommodate to anyone else today. My lioness wouldn't let me.

"What do you want to see?" Shelby asked.

"Two things for sure. The Eiffel Tower and Notre Dame Cathedral. Then I just want to wander and look."

"Okay. I'll go to the Eiffel Tower with you. I've been before, but it's fun to go up in the elevator, and the view from the top is cosmic. I think I'll skip Notre Dame. Once was enough for that."

Shelby was right: the view from the top of the Eiffel Tower was cosmic, what I could see of it through the hordes of tourists speaking different languages and exuding different smells, elbowing their ways to the best viewing spots.

"Okay," Shelby said once we were back on the ground, walking across the Champ-de-Mars, "I'm going. See you later."

"Where are you going?" I asked.

She shrugged. "Anywhere. Want to come?"

For a moment I was tempted, but I knew what I really wanted was to be alone. Or, not alone, but with myself.

"Thanks," I said. "I think I'll go solo."

"Okay. Later, then." She made her way off through the formal garden.

With the pressure of the hard, hot French sun on

the back of my neck, I watched her go. Tomorrow night I'd sleep in my own bed, without Shelby across the room. By then would she, and this garden, and all of Paris seem like a dream, as unreal as Diane the Ever-Beautiful's faraway life?

Notre Dame was full of tourists, some of them talking so loud I wanted to go up to them and say right in their faces, "S-h-h-h-h! This is a church!"

Amazingly, in the midst of all the noise and the constant shuffling sound of moving feet, people still knelt in the chapels and in the nave, saying their prayers. The rich glow of color from the stained-glass windows fell in splashes on the old stonework and lit the faintly damp-smelling air.

I took a seat in the nave and tried to soak in the feel of the place, to find its peace. I sat there for a long time, feeling the weight of the past.

Everyone else was already back by the time I returned to the hotel. "Hi," I said, and waved vaguely in the direction of Ace and Paula in the sitting room before I went into my bedroom, closing the door on my father's "Berkeley . . ."

Shelby was standing over her suitcase, open on the bed. The contents were a jumble of black and white.

"Packing?" I asked. "Already?"

Shelby looked up. She didn't exactly smile, but her face looked pleasant and relaxed. "I know. Boredom, I guess. How was your day?"

214

"Good. Yours?"

She nodded. "Okay. I went to see Jim Morrison's grave."

"Oh, yeah. I forgot he was buried here. How was it?"

Before she could answer, there was a knock on the door and she yelled, "Yeah?"

The door opened and my father stuck his head in. "What do you ladies want to do for dinner tonight? We should do something special for our last night."

I turned to the closet to get my suitcase.

"Why don't you and Mother be the ones to do something special," Shelby said. "You haven't had much time alone together." I turned to look at her. "Berkeley and I can get room service or go out in the neighborhood. You two do it up right."

"No," he said. "We want you with us."

"Go on," Shelby said. "You know you want to."

"Berkeley?" he said, looking at me.

"Fine," I said. "Shelby and I'll have hamburgers or something. You two can do it in style. Wear your tux."

"Well," he said hesitantly. "If that's what you want."

We said it was and he closed the door.

After Ace and Paula left for dinner, I put on the white dress I'd worn on the Seine with Spike and went into the bathroom to brush my hair. When I came out, Shelby was standing in the middle of the room wearing a plain black dress, plain black flats, her Celtic cross, and her paisley scarf. Her hair was brushed and shining and she had on lip gloss and a self-conscious expression.

"Wow," I said.

"You really think so?" Her voice was embarrassed and pleased.

"I'll say. You look sensational." I circled Shelby and she looked good from every angle.

"I went to the Galleries Lafayette this afternoon."

"What's that?"

"A big department store. That's where I got the shoes and the dress."

"How come?"

Shelby shrugged, and apparently that was all the answer I was going to get. Often on this trip I'd felt as if I was looking through a kaleidoscope: the smallest turn and the broken glass pieces arranged themselves into a new pattern which I didn't have time to get used to before it changed again. Shelby was trying something new for her own mysterious reasons. This experimental Shelby was appealing.

"We're not going to settle for any old hamburgers tonight with you looking like that," I said. "Come on." I picked up my own scarf and we set off to find the perfect place for dinner.

We located it on a narrow side street, a tiny Italian restaurant with an outrageously handsome young
216   waiter whose service was attentive and then some.

And while we ate, the new Shelby asked me good questions: Did I mind being an only child? How would I feel if Lily married again? What did Lily and I fight about? I answered as well as I could, because how else could she get to know me?

"What'll you do for the rest of the summer?" I asked Shelby as we walked back to the hotel.

"Camp. Can you believe somebody my age goes to camp? But I always have and it's better than hanging around them for the rest of the summer."

"What do you do at camp?" I remembered Girl Scout Camp, the only sleep-away camp I'd ever been to: eating s'mores around a campfire, taking nature hikes, and making unidentifiable crafts out of pipe cleaners and acorns and paper plates. I couldn't imagine Shelby doing any of those things.

"Not much. Everything's optional, so I don't have to do anything. I play some tennis, get a tan, read. I like to take one of the canoes and go off by myself."

"Do you see the same people every summer there?"

"Some. Nobody special. I kind of like it. No hassles."

We arrived at the hotel and Shelby stopped on the sidewalk outside. I stopped, too. There was something expectant about her. She cleared her throat. "I'm glad you came," she said.

"So am I," I said.

Shelby took a box out of her pocket and thrust it at me. "Here."

"What's this?" I asked, taking it.

217

"A souvenir, that's all."

I opened the box in the light that spilled from the hotel windows. Inside was a gold bracelet with charms of Paris dangling from it: an Eiffel Tower, an Arc de Triomphe, a fleur-de-lis, a French poodle, a bottle of wine, a picture frame with a tiny Mona Lisa in it, a loaf of bread. It was a perfect combination of sentiment and tackiness.

"I love it," I said. "No PTA president should be without one."

"I shouldn't have said that. You can wear it with your cashmere sweater. I got myself one, too."

"We have a lot of matching things now," I said.

"Yeah," Shelby said and looked at her feet. "I guess we should go in."

"I guess. Thank you. *Merci.*"

Shelby shrugged and we went into the hotel.

23

The next morning was a flurry of activity as we packed, had breakfast, made phone calls, paid the bill, and loaded into the limousine for the trip to the airport. I had no time alone with my father and wanted none, though I felt him watching me. All I wanted was a quick goodbye in the Los Angeles airport and a future of guarded and infrequent visits with him, the same as I'd had in the past. Only, this time, I would like it that way.

Once again we flew for an interminable time, with the light outside the window having nothing to do with whatever real time it was inside my body. Meals and movies, snatched naps and the endless throbbing drone of the plane's engines blurred in my head, behind my scratchy eyes, into unreality.

Somehow Shelby was again able to sleep the whole time, and Paula read from a thick paperback novel with an embracing man and woman on the cover. Ace was restless, walking up and down the aisles, reading half a magazine before casting it aside, rummaging in his briefcase, taking his headphones off and on. I had chosen the window seat this time, so he couldn't easily talk to me across Shelby's sleeping body, though he tried. I held my finger to my lips to quiet him, but whispering was impossible over the noise of the plane. He turned irritably away and paced the aisles again.

By the time we reached L.A., I felt as if I could write a book on jet lag. Lack of sleep always made me feel like crying, and being so close to home enforced that feeling.

We stood in a weary huddle waiting for our luggage so we could clear customs. Soon I could get onto another plane and be in San Diego in time to have dinner with Lily.

My father and I passed easily through customs, but, for unknown reasons, the inspectors detained Shelby and Paula. They wanted to conduct a thorough search of their luggage. Perhaps Shelby's stern look and leather jacket made her look like a smuggler.

220   My father was uncharacteristically docile, making

no outraged protests on their behalf. "Why don't you two go get a cup of coffee or something?" Paula said. "Who knows how long this might take. We don't want Berkeley to miss her plane waiting on us."

"All right," Ace said. "We'll be in the departure-area coffee shop."

We walked in silence to the coffee shop, sat, and ordered. Then my father looked at me. "Well," he said and gave me a counterfeit smile. "Party's over."

"Yes."

He looked down at his hands playing with the silverware. "We did a lot."

"Yes, we did," I agreed.

The waitress brought our coffee and we spent longer than necessary adding cream and sugar.

He took a deep breath. "Berkeley, what happened at the end there, I—"

I held up my hand. "I understand what you did, and even why, I think. But I'll never like it, no matter what you say."

"I didn't do anything so awful," he said. "This was our trip. I had a right to expect you to spend your time with *me*."

I shrugged and silently thanked Shelby for demonstrating to me the numerous nuances of that gesture. "I didn't see it that way," I said wearily. "I'd have liked to make my own choice."

"Berkeley, I'm sorry. I don't know how to be with you. You have to help me."

I felt the impulse to soften and steeled myself against it. He was trying again to make the solution mine, wanting me to feel sorry for him, and guilty. Or was he? Maybe he meant what he said. How could I ever be sure?

It was odd, after so many years of feeling something important was missing because I didn't know my father, I still felt that way.

"I don't think I can," I said. I felt the calm, sure strength of my lioness and realized that lately she'd been around more than my rabbit. I should probably give my father credit for that, and be grateful to him.

"I don't give up so easily," he said, and I could see him welcome the renewed challenge of me, another opportunity for Take Charge, Inc. It occurred to me that my elusiveness made me more interesting to him, though that wasn't my intent.

Being with him might always be like a visit to a foreign country: equally interesting and frustrating, with language problems and souvenirs—some treasures, some trash—with the hope that the next visit would be easier, though it would likely only have different pleasures and disappointments.

I looked at my watch. "I better go. I don't want to miss my plane."

My father stood up. "I'll say goodbye to Paula and Shelby for you. They must still be hung up in customs."

We left the coffee shop and walked down the concourse to the boarding gate. I wanted to run.

My flight was called and I looked up at my father. "Thank you for taking me on this trip. I'll never forget it. I learned a lot."

"I wish I knew how you meant that," he said. Unexpectedly, he grabbed me and held me close to him. I was afraid I would cry. I squeezed my burning eyes closed and hugged him back as hard as I could.

"Oh, I'm glad we caught you," Paula's voice said behind me. "I thought we'd never get out of there."

My father released me and I turned to Paula and Shelby, blinking rapidly.

"I know you'll be coming to see us soon," Paula said, taking both my hands in her own, "so I won't say goodbye, just *au revoir*. Until I see you again." She leaned forward and kissed my cheek, then released my hands.

Shelby and I stood looking at each other and suddenly we both grinned at the same time.

"Come see me at school," I said. "We can wear our charm bracelets."

"And our cashmere sweaters," she said, "and our socks."

We didn't touch each other, but I somehow felt we had.

I turned my back on them all and went to my plane.

24

$\mathscr{F}$orty-five minutes later, the plane touched down in San Diego. The hillsides looked brown and dry after the green of France and England, and the sun, even at seven on a summer evening, hit the waters of the Pacific in a wide sparkling swathe.

I didn't care what it looked like, didn't care if the whole city had been paved over while I'd been gone. It was where I wanted to be more than I ever wanted to be anywhere.

Lily was there, waiting, holding a bunch of silver Welcome Home balloons in one hand and a bouquet of flowers in pink tissue paper in the other. As soon as she saw me she ran to me, grabbed me, hugging hard, tangling balloons and flowers behind my back.

"Don't cry, baby, don't cry," Lily said, stroking my rumpled hair with a hand still holding the balloon strings.

Lily's own eyes were wet and I said, "You, too," and we both laughed and dug in our pockets for Kleenex.

We waited for the luggage to come to the carousel, leaning against each other, buoyant and beaming. Lily said, "Thank you for sending me the postcards. I'd thought it would be wonderful to hear from you every day, but the first one took so long to come, and then they came sporadically, and out of order, and there are probably more to arrive. They were more confusing than anything."

"They were hard to write. You can't say enough on a postcard."

"I must say, the ones I got made me want to ask a lot of questions. The wife and stepdaughter went *with* you?"

"Oh, yes, and that was just the beginning."

"You don't have to tell me anything, you know."

"Oh, Lily, don't give me that," I said, joggling her with my elbow. "You're dying to know every single teeny detail."

"I guess you really didn't forget me," she said, laughing. "Well, sure, I'd love to hear it all, but I

225

don't want to pry. Or at least I'll try to restrain myself from prying. I know you won't let me get away with it anyway."

What a relief it was to be with somebody as honest as Lily. I'd even missed her Eye of Doom.

"Mitzi and Nell and Grady wanted to come with me," Lily said as we loaded my bags into the car, "but I wouldn't let them. I wanted you all to myself for a while. Are you exhausted?"

"I was, but I feel fine now."

We got in the car with the silver balloons bobbing around our heads. Lily put the key in the ignition and then stopped. "Oh, God, I can't help myself. Could you just tell me a little of what she's like?"

"Her name's Paula. She wears elegant clothes and makes better small talk than anybody I ever heard. But I'd rather spend five minutes with you than a month with her. I never heard her laugh once."

"Thanks," Lily said. "Can you say anything to me about him?" She started the car.

"Well, I can understand better why you fell in love with him. He's still handsome and charming and fun to be with. Sometimes. And he still likes first-class. You know how you worried that someday he'd come along and get my love without doing anything to earn it?"

"Yes?" Lily said carefully.

"You don't need to worry. He has to earn it."

"What about the future?" Lily still sounded cautious.

"You once said love had a lot to do with being willing to keep muddling along together. He and I don't muddle well. We might learn to, I suppose, but probably not."

"Well, he and I didn't either. What about the step-daughter?"

"Now there's a story."

When we got home, the phone was ringing. Lily unlocked the door and I ran to the kitchen to answer it.

"Berkeley!" Mitzi screamed. "You're back! Oh, thank goodness. Yogurt City has been the pits without you. How was it? Did he buy you lots of things? Did you see Spike? Did you see him in Paris? Oh, don't even tell me. I don't want to hear about how romantic it was. I met somebody while you were gone. I don't know if my name is on his frontal lobe, but there's definitely some chemistry. Or more like electricity. Is that the same thing? Something scientific is going on anyway. Maybe it's biology."

I leaned against the wall and listened, feeling my life open to take me in again as Madge and Wuffums twined around my ankles.

When I finally hung up, I gathered both cats into my arms and joined Lily upstairs. She stood at the doorway to my room, looking in at the clean and tidy surfaces, the tautly made bed.

"I want you to get in there and mess it up," Lily said. "I hate the way it looks without you in it."

"No problem. Come see what I brought you."

We sat together on my bed with the cats tiptoeing on and around us while I gave Lily the scarf from the Sixth Dimension, and the socks. Then I showed her the blue cashmere sweater and the scarf with the pink roses and Shelby's charm bracelet and Grady's snail belt.

"Oh, that's perfect," she said. "He'll be thrilled."

"You and Grady didn't happen to, you know, pay a visit to the Elvis Presley Wedding Chapel in the last two weeks, did you?"

"Sorry, no. But he's coming for dinner tomorrow. How's that?"

"Inadequate, but acceptable. I have a historical factoid for him about Henri II and Diane de Poitiers."

"Well, I'm impressed, and I know he will be."

When we finally finished talking and unpacking, it was almost eleven and exhaustion hit me like a hammer. "I have to go to bed," I told Lily. "Now."

"But you never had anything to eat. Aren't you hungry?"

"You're right. I'm starved. Too starved to sleep." I stood up and swayed with weariness and hunger.

"I'll fix you something," Lily said, getting up, too.

"Stop acting like June Cleaver. I can do it myself. Go to bed. You have to get up early tomorrow and I don't."

"Sure?"

"Sure."

"You want me to take the cats?"

"No. I want them both with me all night, fleas and shedding and everything."

I hugged Lily good night and went downstairs to the kitchen.

Before I opened the refrigerator door, I knew exactly what I would find there. Rolls of film, half-empty cans of cat food, furry leftovers of unidentified origin, as well as the ancient bottle of chutney, a jar of peanut butter, some apples. No beautiful surprises of things I didn't like or want. No hams with pineapple rings, no aspic salads on flowered plates, no apricot mousse in fluted cups—the things I imagined my father would have.

Just Lily's ordinary refrigerator contents—familiar, imperfect, and real. I knew that if Spike had his own refrigerator, it would look just the same.